CSI:

CRIME SCENE INVESTIGATION™

NEVADA ROSE

a novel

Jerome Preisler

Based on the hit CBS series "CSI: Crime Scene Investigation" produced by CBS PRODUCTIONS, a business unit of CBS Broadcasting Inc.

in association with Jerry Bruckheimer Television.

Executive Producers: Jerry Bruckheimer, Carol Mendelsohn, Anthony E. Zuiker, Ann Donahue, Naren Shankar, Cynthia Chvatal, William Petersen, Jonathan Littman

Series created by: Anthony E. Zuiker

POCKET **STAR** BOOKS

New York   London   Toronto   Sydney

Pocket Star Books
A Division of Simon & Schuster, Inc.
1230 Avenue of the Americas
New York, NY 10020

This book is a work of fiction. Names, characters, places, and incidents either are products of the author's imagination or are used fictitiously. Any resemblance to actual events or locales or persons, living or dead, is entirely coincidental.

First Pocket Star Books paperback edition July 2008

POCKET STAR BOOKS and colophon are registered trademarks of Simon & Schuster, Inc.

For information about special discounts for bulk purchases, please contact Simon & Schuster Special Sales at 1-800-456-6798 or business@simonandschuster.com.

Cover design by Richard Yoo; photo of Morganite by John Veevaert, Trinity Minerals

Manufactured in the United States of America

10 9 8 7 6 5 4 3 2 1

ISBN-13: 978-1-4165-4499-9
ISBN-10:   1-4165-4499-2

For Suzanne, again, always.

Never spit in the fire. It will draw your lungs up.
                    —Cajun proverb

Prologue

HE SAT IN the dimness of the room with his third glass of whiskey, the blinds drawn over the windows, their slats tightly shut. He didn't want light seeping through the slats, didn't want any brightness from outside tracking across the walls to remind him how long he'd been out.

The radio was on. Sometimes when he was alone and undisturbed, and there was only the music, listening to the radio would relax him.

Last night was bad, the worst he could ever have imagined, and now a headache was coming on along with the unavoidable dawn, and he was hoping the soft sounds would help keep it from getting out of control. He liked the ballad that was playing—it was a popular love song, he'd heard it everywhere around. It usually put him off, those bombardments. The sort that came when you were driving or hurrying to get through the store. When you were wherever you happened to be, going wherever you were going, and needed silence more than anything else in the world.

There was a time and a place for music. When you didn't want it, it could turn into a hateful thing. But this song was different . . . even at the wrong time, in the wrong places, he'd found that its words and melody had caught his ear. The singer's voice . . . the emotion pouring out of it, the anguish . . .

Nina Tyford. That was her name.

Her voice had gotten to him, touched something inside him. And right now, he was hoping it helped.

Along with the whiskey.

"First line," he said into the black. "Cortisone, Verapamil, lithium. Whiskey, Nina Tyford, Angel Heart."

His eyes closed, the tension behind them packed into a tight, pulsing ball. He swallowed what was in his glass, reached across his armrest for the bottle, poured another drink, and then listened to the soft, sad music on the radio.

Angel . . . Angel . . . Angel . . .
You always call me Angel
But I don't know why
You never understand me
No matter how hard I try

Keeping his head very still, he held his glass out in front of him and moved it rhythmically in the dimness. Back and forth like a conductor, back and forth, with some up and down for effect till a little whiskey sloshed over the rim of the glass—not much, but enough to put a spot of wetness on the base of his thumb.

He pulled the drink in toward his lips, licked off what was on his hand.

"Second line," he said. "Sansert, Depakote, triptans, whiskey. Sing to me, Nina Tyford."

He emptied the glass again and listened.

Loving you is easy
And I know you love me too
There are moments, passing moments,
When it shows in the little things you do

Still in my heart's a sorrow
I'd thought that time would fade
Guess it's the kind of love you give
The kind of love we've made

He reached for the bottle again, filled up. When the episodes reached their cyclic peak, nothing usually remedied them better than the whiskey. That, soft music, and now his singing girl on the radio. And after last night . . . after last night, God, how he needed her beautiful voice and her song. Nina Tyford almost made him believe there were women somewhere who could feel as deeply as he felt. Women who knew how to give love the way he'd always given it.

Given, and given, loving his woman to death without ever getting enough in return.

"Nina Tyford, I want to think you'd understand," he said. "I want to think you would, I truly do. DHE, intranasal cocaine drops, whiskey. Third line."

A cold little chuckle, and he went back to his conducting.

A love of pain and pleasure, a love that
lasts forever
Open up your heart to me

Angel . . . Angel . . . Angel . . .

Why not change it all tomorrow, free our love
from sorrow?
Open up your heart to me

He sloshed some whiskey around in his mouth, swallowed, reached for the bottle, poured again. How many would this make? Four drinks? Five? He'd lost count, but what did it matter? He didn't have to go anywhere, and wasn't going anywhere he didn't have to. For today, and maybe longer, he was staying put.

And for a few minutes more, at least, he would have Nina and her song.

Angel . . .Angel . . . Angel . . .
You always call me Angel
But I don't know why
You never understand me
No matter how hard I try

He suddenly felt a sharp, crackling bolt of pain between his temples and sat up straight even as the music began its gradual fade-out.

"Fourth line," he said. "Nina Tyford, please, shit. *Fourth line.*"

But there was no fourth line for him, and he knew much better than to expect it. He had nothing now but the whiskey that had failed him without warning and the last traces of Nina Tyford's refrain drifting off in the reinforced dimness of the room.

Nothing but nothing but nothing.

And next up on the radio, a song he didn't want to hear.

He whimpered miserably, tossed the glass from his hand, and heard the jagged sound of it breaking against the wall, shattering the way his head felt it would at any moment. As he doubled over at the edge of the seat cushion, he covered the upper part of his face with his hand, so he could hardly breathe, pressing his thumb and forefinger deep into his tightly shut eyelids.

Pressing his fingers in until it hurt, then pressing harder, wondering if he could keep it up till the awful pain matched his headache or he'd punched his eyeballs back out of their sockets.

He would take whichever came first, having finally learned one thing about life.

Call it a lesson, call it a basic fact: You could choose your pleasures and your remedies but never your punishments.

1

A TABLETOP ALTAR stood in the corner just inside Rose Demille's bedroom door, draped in a deep blue satin cloth accented by a pleated valance. In the center of the cloth, an extinguished yellow votive candle, delicately scented with honeysuckle, had almost melted down to the socket of its polished brass holder.

As he entered the room a step or two behind Catherine Willows, Warrick Brown paused to regard a framed portrait of Saint Peter on the wall above the altar. Somehow, its presence there surprised him, though, considering the victim's background, he could not have explained why.

After a moment, Warrick turned toward the bed, where the woman known from one end of town to another as "Nevada" Rose Demille lay sprawled atop her sheets, her sightless gaze fixed on the ceiling, her arms and legs tied to her bed-posts, the posts appearing to be made of the same shiny orange brass as the candlestick on the meditative altar near the door.

Crouched over the body, Dave Phillips, the assistant coroner, was busy fishing around in his medical examiner's field kit. Warrick moved deeper into the room behind Catherine, readied his camera, and waited. He could hear the maid wailing out in the driveway with Jim Brass, but if the picture of the saint had caught him off guard, her carrying on was very easy to explain.

Warrick knew there was a good chance of hysterics whenever anybody stumbled on a corpse, anyway. Mariah Valley was a swank master-planned community about fifteen miles from the Strip, and this was among its most exclusive sections. The affluent residents of these neighborhoods tended to have domestic help—maids, pool keepers, gardeners, fitness coaches, personal cooks, and so forth. When the vics lived alone, as Rose apparently had, it wasn't unusual for their bodies to be discovered by a hired hand. Pay someone to show up at a certain time every day, and he or she was more liable to do so than your loving husband or mother.

For Warrick Brown, the odds were the thing. Not the stacked odds of the casino floor but legit statistical probabilities. There were always mathematical predictors for evaluating people's behavior—and the fewer variables involved, the easier it was to calculate how the dice would roll. The record downpour of a couple of weeks ago had been a significant X factor, giving Las Vegans all sorts of reasons to get sidetracked in their everyday lives. But Warrick had observed that money was a great equalizer when it came to remembering obligations and appointments . . . even for someone struggling to bail out from under the floodwaters that had turned entire suburban neighborhoods into soggy river deltas.

Now Warrick and Catherine continued waiting for Dave to wrap up his exam of Nevada Rose's bound, gagged, completely naked, and admittedly still very beautiful body. Dave manipulated her wrists and ankles, wobbled the lower jaw, and lifted an eyelid over a filmy pupil with his latex-gloved fingertip.

"There's mild rigor mortis," he announced without looking up from the corpse.

Warrick not only got the sense that Dave was talking to himself, but also had a feeling he was unaware anyone else had even joined him. He watched the coroner in silence a moment, and then let his gaze drift around the room.

Besides the altar and the bed, its furnishings consisted of a dresser, a nightstand, and a large antique cane chair. Telephone on the stand, a ceramic bowl on the dresser. The bowl was the color of red earth, with a simple blue decorative pattern on the outer surface. Warrick thought it was Native American . . . possibly Shoshone or one of the other local tribes.

He went over to see what, if anything, it contained and found only loose odds and ends—the kind of stuff Rose might have emptied from her pockets or picked up off the rug, tossed into the bowl meaning to either discard or put them away afterward, and then promptly forgot about.

Carefully shifting the various items around with a latexed finger, Warrick noticed several AA batteries, an unopened package of sugarless chewing gum, a pencil with a broken point, a thin red leather watchband, paper clips, a cigarette lighter, a square of yellow Post-its, and a few dollars worth of mixed change. Also, partially buried under the rest of the bowl's contents was one of those pill dispensers with reminder features that were used for everything from prescription medications to daily multiple vitamins.

Warrick lifted the dispenser from the bowl, snapped it open, and found nothing inside. Considering all the junk that had been scattered on top of it, he doubted it had been used recently. If drugs had contributed to Rose Demille's death, they probably wouldn't have come from this pillbox. Still, it might pay to find out what it had contained.

He bagged it in a Ziploc before turning to check on Dave's progress.

All signs were that he'd moved right along. Reaching into his kit for a digital thermometer,

Dave had raised the body slightly onto one hip, inserted the rectal probe, and held its nonbusiness end steady in his hand. A series of electronic beeps, then he checked the temperature.

"Her core's ninety-three-point-nine degrees Fahrenheit," he said, reading the display. "Couple that with the rigor and lividity of the extremities, and I'd estimate she's been dead around two hours."

Warrick checked his watch. It was nine A.M. on the dot.

"One, two, three o'clock, four o'clock rock," he said to Catherine.

She looked at him and gave a thin smile. Dave, meanwhile, seemed about finished with the DB. He carefully extracted his probe, cleaned it with an antibacterial wipe, stuffed the wipe into a plastic zip bag, closed the kit, and rose to his feet

"She's all yours, " he said, finally acknowledging the criminalists. "I've gotta get back. See you guys later." And with that, he headed out the door.

"Later, Dave," Catherine called out.

The CSIs went about their work, Catherine going around the bed toward the victim, Warrick raising his camera for a series of snapshots. Though he wasn't inclined to be judgmental about how Rose had conducted her life, he'd pretty much ruled out the possibility of her being canonized in death like the guardian of her altar. No candidate for sainthood would boast a rose tattoo on her shapely—and to all appearances implant-free—right breast. Nor was a saint-in-progress likely to have worn the sheer robe that had been haphazardly tossed over an arm of the living-room sofa. Or the pair of stiletto heels outside the bedroom door. Or the skimpy thong panties Warrick had seen on the carpet near the foot of the bed.

"It'd be very quiet here so early in the morning," Catherine said, turning to him. "If any of the neighbors were awake and about, they might have noticed someone running out the door around that time."

"Or heard someone go barrelling down the road at ninety miles an hour."

"Assuming our certain someone didn't stick around to admire Rose after she died."

Warrick nodded. They had left Jim Brass out front taking the housekeeper's statement, part of which related to a gym bag she'd found on the lawn alongside the garage. According to her, it was there when she arrived for work, and her first thought was that the driver of a car might have dropped it while hurrying off. This had given her a nervous feeling, though she wouldn't in a million years have expected what she discovered *inside* the house.

Warrick fell into thoughtful silence. At the bedside, Catherine had put down her kit and knelt over the body. In her black field vest, black jeans, and latex surgical gloves, she might have been a cross between a SWAT cop and a medical doctor on house call.

"Her lips have a slight bluish discoloration. Also, I see petechial hemorrhaging," she said, indicating the pinpoint blood spots in the whites of Rose's eyes.

Both were characteristic signs of hypoxia.

Warrick shifted his camera lens onto the dead woman's hands and feet. It was important to get abundant photo documentation of the ropes binding them to the posts, since they'd be cut and bagged as evidence before Rose was wheeled into the morgue wagon. The placement of the knots— and the way they were tied—could reveal a lot about whoever had done the tying. Particularly if what they were seeing here turned out to have similarities with other crime scenes.

"There any ligature marks on the throat?" he asked.

Catherine shook her head, her gaze suddenly a bit distant. "No superficial bruises on the body, either."

Warrick clicked away. Her expression told him she was visualizing how Rose's final moments could have gone down, the images flickering across the screen of her mind. All of the lab's veteran criminalists got that remote look in their eyes from time to time—and came to recognize it in one another.

"Could be Rose was having a sexual role-playing fantasy that went too far," she said.

Warrick nodded, thinking along with her. "Then her partner flees in a panic after realizing *how* far it went."

"Yeah," Catherine said. "Look around this place."

Warrick assumed she was being rhetorical. They'd done that together during their walk-through and observed nothing to indicate forced entry at the doors or windows. Nothing whatsoever broken or disturbed in the room. And no fingernail scrapings that pointed toward a struggle. Furthermore, the scattered locations of Rose's robe, heels, and panties suggested she'd voluntarily shed them—or let someone undress her—on the way from the living room to the bedroom.

"BDSM games." Warrick lifted the camera to his eye. "Seems . . . plausible."

Catherine picked up on his uncertain tone, tilted her head.

"Except . . . ?"

"I've seen people who've died from oxygen deprivation while taking hot licks in the sack," he said. His lens whirred, auto-focusing. "It mostly happens when a victim's been hog-tied on his or her stomach. With your hands and feet restrained behind your back, the abdominal muscles tire out, and it gets harder and harder to breathe."

"Until you stop," Catherine said.

Warrick nodded, pressed his shutter button a few times.

Clickclickclick.

Moving around the bed now, Catherine took her ultraviolet flashlight from a belt holster, snapped an amber filter behind its head, and thumbed it on. She ran the beam slowly over Rose's thighs, then onto the sheets between them, searching for obvious stains from semen or vaginal secretions. It helped that the shades were drawn—the dimmer the room, the easier it would be to detect UV fluorescence.

"She might've been using narcotics or alcohol," Catherine mulled aloud. "Or she could have had a preexisting health condition. Heart disease, asthma, bronchitis . . . any one of those could lead to her suffocating in this position."

She paused and studied the bedding through the filter.

"Well?" Warrick said. "Anything?"

"No."

Warrick shrugged. "Her romantic evening might've gone bad before the real fun and games started."

Catherine didn't answer. She had returned the flashlight to its case and produced a hand magnifier from a vest pouch. Warrick lowered his camera and went over to where she squatted. Maybe there'd been no sex stains, but it was clear that something had caught her attention.

She looked at him, motioning toward a rumpled wedge of top sheet between the dead woman's bare thighs.

"Blond hairs," he said.

"But not naturally blond." She passed him the magnifier.

Warrick peered through the lens, grunted. "Lower down the follicle, the color's more a sandy brown."

"They've been frosted," Catherine said. "And it doesn't match our victim."

He nodded his understanding. Spilled across her pillowcase in disarray, Rose's tresses were long, thick, and uniformly chestnut brown. Even a quick look at the hairs under the lens revealed them to be a different texture and color.

He moved aside as Catherine collected the hair samples with her tweezers and deposited them in a small glassine envelope.

"I wonder if the lightener's a professional or consumer brand?" she said. "If it's a salon product, that'd definitely help with—"

"You two might want another look at this."

The interruption jerked their attention toward the half-open door, where Captain Jim Brass had suddenly appeared with the gym bag recovered from the front lawn—a navy blue nylon duffel with the Nike swoosh on its side. Warrick realized he could no longer hear the maid carrying on outside.

"We miss something before?" he said.

Brass entered, holding the gym bag with one hand, displaying a small, flat object in his opposite palm.

"One of the uniforms found this ID tag in a hedge a few feet from the driveway. Looks like its fastener might've snagged on a branch and gotten torn off the duffel's zipper."

Catherine stood up and looked it over.

"Mark Baker," she said, reading the name penned under the clear plastic window.

Brass seemed disappointed at her lack of immediate familiarity with it. Dressed nattily in a dark gray suit with a polished detective's badge on the lapel, he was a broad, stocky man with a receding hairline, features as blunt as his typical disposition, and eyes that had seen it all far too often.

Just at that moment, those eyes jumped off Catherine to land on Warrick's face.

"How about you? Name ring a bell?"

Warrick's brow creased thoughtfully.

"Fireball," he said.

"*The* Fireball, right."

"Wait a minute," Catherine said with dawning recognition. "Isn't that some baseball player's handle?"

"Might be the greatest lefty pitcher ever," Warrick said, nodding. "He's also got a rep for being a ladies' man . . ."

"They've been spotted together around town," Brass said. "Nevada Rose and Baker. As a couple." He looked at Warrick. "My guess is I'm not telling you anything you don't know."

Warrick was silent. The captain was one of

the straightest shooters he'd met on the job and didn't waste time getting to the point.

No stranger to the Vegas nightlife, Warrick had once come close to signing with a minor league baseball team—an interest in the game stuck with him long after he enrolled in college. By that time, though, he'd already realized that betting on pro sports (and coming up a winner) was a much quicker and easier way to make his tuition than waiting tables.

"I heard they were an item," Warrick said after a moment. "There were stories that they were ready to tie the knot. No pun intended." He shrugged. "Who knows what's true? It isn't like I sit around watching those entertainment shows. Or like they're known for their high standards of reporting."

"But Rose had a relationship with him," Brass persisted.

Warrick didn't know why he suddenly felt defensive. "This woman had a whole *lot* of relationships. She was known as a maneater . . ."

"Famous athletes having been her favorite menu item."

Warrick looked at him but said nothing.

"Do what you need to in here. I'm going to have this gym bag tagged as evidence and make some phone calls," Brass said. "We'll want an expanded perimeter around the crime scene. And added uniformed details for when the carny train rolls up and clowns start spilling out all over the goddamned place."

Warrick and Catherine exchanged meaningful looks, then watched Brass turn on his heels and stride heavily out the door.

"I don't blame him," Warrick finally said. "He sees what's coming. The media's going to be at this with steak knives and barbecue sauce."

Catherine kept looking at him but didn't say anything.

"I heard Rose Demille was from New Orleans," Warrick said. "Last of a high-stepping family line. After Katrina, she loaded up her good looks and expensive tastes and moved to Vegas."

"Fabulous Las Vegas, that is," Catherine said. "Swimmin' pools, sports superstars."

Warrick smiled soberly. "Rose chased players," he said. "Their big-time lifestyles, their bank accounts—"

"And their hard bodies," Catherine said.

"Yeah," Warrick said. "Them, too, I suppose."

Their eyes met.

"You *do* know stuff about her," Catherine said.

"Some." Warrick rubbed his light scruff of beard. "Of all the guys she hooked up with, I figure Mark Baker's got to be the richest and most famous."

"The prize catch, huh?"

Warrick was silent. His gaze had drifted back to the wall above the satin-covered altar, hung with a bland portrait of Christ's second apostle holding the key to heaven against his white-robed breast.

"It's an old-time Creole custom to have an altar and a picture of your patron saint in the bedroom," he said. "A yellow votive candle near the door's supposed to bring people wealth. And Saint Peter with his key's a symbol of quick success. They say he holds the key to everything and opens all doors."

Catherine glanced briefly at the picture, then returned her attention to the nude, lifeless woman on the bed.

"Sure is looking like Nevada Rose opened *her* door to the wrong person," she said.

2

"Wow," Greg Sanders said. "I guess it *really* ain't easy being green."

Gil Grissom adjusted his glasses by the stems. "Is that your empirical scientific assessment or Kermit the Frog's?" he said.

Greg didn't miss his boss's frown of disapproval, its camouflage on a mild baby face notwithstanding. He also saw the simultaneous cautionary glance from Sara Sidle, who briefly turned from her camera's viewfinder to send it in his direction. She'd joined them at the lakeside moments ago, after talking to a group of horrified groundskeepers some yards back near the trees.

Greg dropped his shoulders. The night shift was barely an hour old. No way did he want it getting off on the wrong track.

He gazed out across the water, figuring he'd

give Grissom's annoyance a minute to pass. The Fairmark Resort's man-made lake was pretty large, he thought. Well, actually, very large by local standards. Its basin held, what, fifty million gallons of water? Something close to that, anyway, a volume that would make it about double the size of the artificial lake outside the Bellagio Hotel. Very large, yeah, and establishing a new standard of ecological wastefulness right here in the foothills of a desert mountain range. Greg had to hand it to the resort's developers, though. Nestled amid the slopes with hundreds of feet of elevation change, its new world-class championship golf course—and the lake that was its picturesque centerpiece—represented an impressive feat of engineering and landscaping.

Greg ruffled his short, choppy hair with his fingers, a habit that made him look kind of awkward and even younger than his thirty-four years. Add these qualities to his semi-intentional slouch, and he hoped his body language would transmit on a simultaneously innocent and contrite bandwidth.

He continued staring out at the lake another few seconds. The late-afternoon sun, sputtering in over the craggy western slopes, had fallen over its surface in weak orange patches, and Greg watched its mute swans swim elegantly between and through them. Swimming being a big part of what the birds did. The floater also had been doing what floaters did before getting hauled onto dry land. It was, in fact, first observed drifting among the bevy of swans, which by all accounts had seemed as unaffected by its presence as they were by the dozen or so law-enforcement officers, crime-lab personnel, and Clark County emergency-cleanup volunteers now milling about the lakeside.

Of course, Greg thought, those birds had probably gotten used to circumnavigating foreign objects over the past few days, the floodwaters having washed untold tons of debris off the slopes.

What was the golfer's term for a large body of water? He couldn't nail it and finally left it alone. It would come to him later, he told himself. And besides, Grissom's irritation had visibly passed. He was ready to enter his momentary penitence.

"What I meant to say about this guy a minute ago is that, besides being green all over, he's been dead awhile," Greg said. He cocked a thumb over his shoulder at the group of deputies. "They told us he was level in the water when they found him. His head and arms on the surface."

Down on his knees beside Sara, Gil Grissom nodded his understanding.

Soon after a person died, the methane and other gases in the stomach and intestines formed pockets in the abdomen, in the colon, or up inside the lungs and esophagus. In that state of primary flotation, the head, arms, and torso tended to dip below the surface while the inner body cavities filled with gas. But as progressive decay swelled the body's outer tissues, its buoyancy got more evenly distributed throughout the extremities—a telltale sign of secondary flotation.

That was basic, and far easier than determining their John Doe's rate of decomposition. The amount of time he'd taken to reach his present state depended on what he'd last eaten and drunk before he died, his general health, the lake water's temperature, its mineral, chemical, and organic content . . . a whole checklist of variables had to be considered.

Still, Grissom had been around long enough to know a ripe cadaver when he saw one. Some of the damage had been caused by scavengers picking at its soft tissues—the eyelids, ears, and left nostril were missing, and the upper lip was eaten away to bare the front teeth and gums, giving its open mouth an angry, snarling appearance. But the face was also bloated from advancing putrefaction, and the skin had begun to slough off the bones of its macerated hands like thin, moist gloves.

Besides which, all three CSIs could smell the odor of human rot.

Ignoring the stench now, Grissom looked intently into the dead man's blind, lidless eyes. They were protruding from their sockets, and the breakdown of red blood cells had given them a cloudy, whitish appearance. Their outer surfaces were flattened—Grissom couldn't help but think

of failed poached eggs. Not an appetizing comparison, but not awful, either. The flattening would
have occurred as vitreous fluid leaked through
their connective tissues and the layers of the eyeball globes collapsed.

Grissom brought his face closer to the dead
man's, grunted. The lens of the left eye had de-
tached and slipped down below the iris—more
connective tissue decay. But he'd noticed something else of particular interest.

He got an ophth scope out of his kit and took a
closer look. "I see a horizontal line," he said. "Between the cornea and sclera. Both eyes."

Sara knelt there with her booted toes pressing into the muddy embankment. The ground
squished under them when she shifted her
weight.

"The front of the eyeball had a chance to dry
out," she said, picturing it exposed to air through
a partially raised lid. "You think he died on land?"

Grissom pointed to the dead man's fingers.
They were outspread, their skin loose and sloughy
like the formalin-preserved skin teased from a
specimen frog.

"A drowning person will grasp at plants, reeds,
clots of bottom muck . . . there's an instinc-
tive impulse to get a handhold even if none is
around," he said. "The clutching motion typically
leaves fingernail marks on the palms."

"And he has none," Sara said.

"No, not of that type," Grissom said. "If he

wound up in water *after* he was killed, the questions become how and when that happened. We don't know his rate of decomposition. But the fish and crustaceans wouldn't have waited to turn him into a buffet course."

"What about this algae on Green Man's face?" Greg motioned toward a flaccid cheek. "He's pretty shaggy . . . it's more than a five o'clock shadow."

Grissom produced another low grunt of concentration. While he wouldn't have put it that way himself, Greg was right. The dead man's exposed head, neck, and hands were covered in prokaryotic fuzz. It would have taken time to spread to that extent and might very well turn out to be all over him—the CSIs still hadn't had a chance to look under his clothing.

Nevertheless . . .

"A lot of microorganisms that used to be considered algae aren't anymore—it's a fairly obsolete term," he said. "What they've got in common is that they all perform photosynthesis. Blue-green algae are closer to bacteria than plants. But hundreds of varieties could thrive in the lake. And more than one could grow on the body. We need to determine the species to know the growth rate."

"I already took a scraping from the film on the back of his hand," Sara said. She handed the ophth scope back to Grissom. "Wouldn't it give us the reproductive patterns and chlorophyll levels?"

"In theory. Although—"

"The lake water's composition would affect the life cycle," Greg volunteered. He took a sample vial from his pocket. "I'm gonna go bottle some for a culture."

Grissom was pleased, his earlier annoyance massaged away. "That'll help," he said.

Sara returned her attention to the floater as Greg started toward the bank. "Have you noticed that he's *glowing*?" she said, raising her camera.

"And not from blissful contentment."

She glanced at Grissom over her shoulder. He took a moment to appreciate her hint of a smile.

"Prokaryotes have iridescent qualities," he said. "As do most related life-forms. Diatoms, for instance, are being biofarmed as pigment ingredients for Day-Glo cosmetics."

"Snazzy."

Grissom shrugged. "The ancient Greeks had a saying: 'Who glows not, burns not.'"

She smiled a little more and went back to taking pictures. "He's wearing work clothes," she said.

Grissom took in the tattersall shirt, the sand-colored cargo pants, the heavy leather gear belt with its oversized pouches. Then he motioned to the boots.

"They look like they're professional quality," he said.

"For hiking or climbing?"

"Maybe." Grissom paused. "We'll check out

their manufacturer—there's a logo on the ankle, see?"

Sara took a shot of the stitched-in lettering and then shuffled around the body for a close-up of the dead man's head.

Her eyebrow suddenly shot up. "I can see a foamy substance in his mouth," she said. "Toward the back of the tongue."

Grissom leaned forward as she got a tongue depressor out of her kit. Everything the body had revealed thus far contradicted a drowning scenario. But a froth of mucus, air, and water would exude from the airway of a victim who'd gasped for breath before going under.

Sara pushed down on the pale, thickened tongue with her right hand, opening the mouth wider with her left.

Her eyebrow rose another tick. "Does this look like a bronchial secretion to you?" she said.

Grissom hesitated. There were tiny whitish specks in the fluid.

"No," he said.

"Doesn't to me, either."

"I think it's an oviparous cluster."

"Eggs?"

He nodded. "If I'm a pregnant fish or amphibian, I find a sheltered hole to lay them in. The dead man's open mouth would make a perfect underwater nursery."

Sara looked at him. "Rock-a-bye baby," she said. "You want a swab from my kit?"

Grissom reached under its open lid for a Magill forceps. "I'll borrow this from you instead, it'll work better." He inserted the instrument's grasping end into the mouth. "Push the tongue down a little more so I can get in there, thanks."

He was capping an evidence tube filled with the fluid when a sheriff's deputy approached with a member of the cleanup crew. They stopped a few feet away, behind the crime-scene tape that had been hastily placed between a couple of police barricades.

Grissom bagged his vial. "Gentlemen," he said. "What can I do for you?"

The cleanup worker stared uneasily at the floater a moment. A beefy man in jeans, waders, and an orange vest, he had his hands stuffed into heavy-duty rubber work gloves.

"I'm Eddie Yost," he said. "A foreman with the Fairmark's grounds crew."

Grissom waited.

"I need to know when you're gonna be done with that thing," Yost said.

Grissom looked at him. "Thing?" he said. "You mean this dead man?"

"Dead guy, stiff, whatever."

Grissom knelt over the body, trying to decide how to answer.

"We're collecting evidence for the LVPD crime lab," he said. "We'll be done when we're done . . . why?"

Yost frowned and gestured toward the group

of men near the trees. "My guys're trying to get this green in shape. And all they can do's hang around this here water hazard till you finish up."

Grissom considered how to answer, found himself at a loss, and did a little more considering. Meanwhile, Greg had come up behind the groundskeeper as he returned with his water sample.

"What were those words you just used?" he asked the foreman.

"You mean 'finish up'?"

"Before that."

Yost looked at him. "Water hazard," he said flatly.

Greg grinned, and looked as if he would have patted Yost's shoulder. "*Right*, that's it. Thank you. Water hazard."

Grissom gave Sara a look. "How appropriate," he said.

3

SHE PHONED AT six o'clock, about the time they usually ate supper. He knew who it was right off the bat, so what if her number was blocked? She'd gotten into the habit of interrupting him as they sat down at the table—it was a jealousy thing.

Tonight, though, he was still on the road when he heard the ring tone.

He took a hand off the steering wheel, lifted his cell out of its dash holder, and flipped it open.

"Yeah?" he said.

"What's going on?" she answered. "She ain't heard from you. Not since this morning."

"Look, calm down."

"Don't talk to me that way. She just tried you at home, and nobody answered."

He frowned. "I'm just drivin' in."

"Now? You've been out all day?"

"Since before the sun came up," he said. "An' here it is dark again."

A pause.

"I swear, she's sick to her heart," she said. "Why didn't nobody answer the phone at your place?"

"If somebody was there, somebody would've picked up."

"She shouldn't have to talk to no machine—"

"Did you hear me? I just said nobody's home there. Everything's been upside down lately. You ain't got to be told that."

Another silence. She was a jealous, possessive bitch when it came to him. Sometimes he hated how good that made him feel. How damn important.

He stepped on the gas, inching up over eighty-five. He knew he'd start hitting traffic maybe ten, fifteen miles up the road as he got closer to the cutoff. But on this stretch, he could go for a long while without seeing another driver's taillights.

"You still there?" she said.

"I'm here."

"Were you up there lookin' for him?"

"All day, like I told you."

"And?"

"She would've heard about it if I found him."

Her frustration came on hard through the phone. "Damn your precious Nevada Rose," she said. "Been nothing but sorrow for me."

"No," he said. "That ain't fair."

"Don't you tell her what's fair. Her heart's been broke."

"But she's talkin' crazy." And he knew there'd be no end to it, not once she got on a rant.

"You listen up," she said. "She loves you. She can say whatever she wants. Not like that other one."

"Why you got to bring her into this?"

"Because others come and go. But you're always gonna be her baby angel. And she needs to know that you love her most."

"She knows."

"If she did, she wouldn't have to ask."

"C'mon. That's more crazy shit—"

"Don't you use that language with me. Crazy this, crazy that. She heard it her whole life, and plenty worse besides. You want to be addin' to her hurt tonight?"

" 'Course not—"

"Then she needs to hear that you love her. Her heart's *broke*."

"Stop. I love her. She knows I love her."

"Most?"

"Most."

"That's better. And she loves her boy. She loves you, and don't ever forget it, no matter what selfish thoughts that other puts in your head."

"I wish she wouldn't start in on that again. I can't stand no more of it."

"You know it's her who's at the root of our troubles. Couldn't even answer the phone—"

"No, stop." The left side of his neck had started to throb. "I wish she'd stop."

"Then do what's right. You promised her somethin'. You put dreams in her head. And now you look at how she suffers."

"It ain't my fault—"

"That Nevada Rose. So special. So perfect. And look. It's you that started this. And it's you alone who has to set things right. Or right's they can be."

"But—"

"You make things right for us," she said. "Please, baby angel, I need you to make things right."

He tried to think of something to say, couldn't, and instead just tossed his phone onto the seat beside him without another word.

Flooring the pedal now, feeling the surge of speed push him back into his seat, he resisted the momentary urge to shut his eyes and keep them shut as he sped on over the dark, empty road.

Catherine Willows entered the morgue room to find Warrick and Al Robbins, the LVPD's chief coroner, conferring over the autopsy slab where Robbins had laid out Rose Demille for his exam.

"Sorry I'm late," she said. "Kid stuff."

Robbins continued talking as the door swung shut behind her.

Catherine approached the slab, looked at the draining cadaver. She could hear the slow, steady drip of blood and other fluids into the sink basin.

A moment ago, she had been on the phone with her teenage daughter, who'd called from school to say she would be home late—and was immediately coy as to the reason why.

Catherine breathed. It was like slipping between different worlds. When one intruded on the other, even briefly, she sometimes found herself a bit jarred from her frame of reference. It rarely happened. And it mostly passed in the scant moment it took her to inhale and exhale—too quickly for anyone to notice. But ever since Lindsey had been kidnapped, snatched from Catherine's car on the way home from dance class, even a budding argument about what she was up to when Mom wasn't around could occasionally prompt Catherine to reflect on the overlap between her normal routines as a woman and mother, and the horrors she saw on the job every day.

Once, after a courtroom appearance that helped convict a serial murderer, she had gone out for a drink with the lead detective on the case. It was a tough, exhausting prosecution for them—not from an evidentiary standpoint but because the victims were young children and their killer had been a mutilator. And because he'd been brutally inventive with his carving tools. Lindsey was in second grade at the time. The detective told her he had eleven-year-old twins.

At the bar, their one drink had turned into several rounds. Between her second and third, Catherine had asked the detective what people who work violent crimes often wonder about one another, and themselves, in somber, reflective moments.

"What makes you want to keep doing it?"

He'd held his Scotch below his lips, slowly blinked his eyes. *"I think of myself as speaking for the dead,"* he had replied. *"It sounds overdramatic, but it's how I feel. I speak for them because they can't speak for themselves."*

He'd paused after that, gulped his drink, and then spun the question back at her.

"How about you, Catherine? What's the pull?"

Catherine was momentarily speechless—it was something Grissom had also said almost verbatim on more than one occasion. Meeting his haunted stare, she'd suddenly clamped down on the answer rising inside her. Her words to him came from no deeper than her vocal cords. *"Plain, simple curiosity,"* she'd said, and quickly started on her cocktail. *"When I get to a crime scene, I just want to know what the hell's happened."*

Catherine wasn't sure why she'd flashed on that recollection right now. But occasionally things sprang into her mind at odd times. She hadn't been candid with the detective, not nearly, and she supposed she regretted it. Considering she'd raised the question in the first place, it had been unfair of her.

"There was no semen, no vaginal trauma, and the initial toxicology results are clean," Robbins was saying. He flipped over a sheet of paper on the clipboard in his right hand and scanned the one beneath it. "A standard multipanel drug test shows alcohol in her bloodstream. But its level is insignificant, less than two-tenths of one percent. No trace amphetamines, barbiturates, benzodiazepines, cocaine, cannabis, methamphetamines, MDMA . . ."

Warrick eyed the chart over Robbins's shoulder. "How far along are the poison batteries?" he said.

"Again, we've excluded the common substances." Robbins glanced up at him, leaning his weight on a metal cane in his left hand. "I can offer an educated guess about the cause of death. Pending the outcome of additional tox screens. And, I suppose, chemical trace testing on the pill dispenser you brought in."

"I'm listening," Warrick said.

"The term *burked* should ring a bell with the two of you? From the Tony Braun murder?"

Catherine nodded. "Old but not forgotten business."

"Older than you might realize—the word has an interesting history." Robbins said. "'Up the close and down the stair, in the house with Burke and Hare.' It's the first line in a nineteenth-century British nursery rhyme. Many of them have dark origins—they were meant to scare the kids into bed."

"And keep them from sneaking back out, I imagine," Catherine said.

Warrick had remembered something. "Whoa. Hang on a second. Weren't Burke and Hare body snatchers?"

"Not quite," Robbins said. "The rhyme tells it all. Body snatchers—or resurrection men—would go to graveyards for their merchandise. But *close* was slang for a narrow hall or alleyway. Burke and Hare found live bodies easier pickings than dead ones. Digging up corpses from under six feet of soil was sweaty work. And their client, a Professor Robert Knox, preferred fresh subjects for his anatomy classes in Edinburgh."

"Sounds like the formula for a lasting business relationship," Catherine said.

"Knox was a member of the Royal Medical Society," Robbins said. "A respected doctor and teacher. In those days, only bodies of executed criminals could be used for human dissections. There were too few to meet the demand."

"So our ghoulish entrepreneurs jumped in to exploit the supply-side shortage."

Robbins gave her a shrug. "I can appreciate Knox's predicament," he said. "Human beings are machines that just happen to have soft, perishable parts."

"Meaning?"

"Doctors sometimes get lost in the workings." He looked at her neutrally a moment. "Burke and Hare murdered sixteen people in less than a year.

While one covered the nose and mouth, his partner would sit on the victim's chest to pin him or her down. Death occurred through smothering and left the bodies with few outward signs of violence. It enabled Knox to have his no-questions-asked policy."

"Or see no evil," Warrick said. "Depending how you look at it."

The coroner's bearded face remained expressionless. "Burke's the butcher, Hare's the thief, Knox the man who buys the beef," he said. "I can imagine myself in the doctor's shoes. It doesn't mean I've got a stake in how posterity treats him."

He shrugged again, his left shoulder rising higher than the right because of how he pressed his weight on the cane. His legs were both prosthetic, the consequence of a terrible accident he rarely ever mentioned. Warrick had long ago noticed he favored the left side and supposed it must give him chronic aches.

Now he watched Robbins go around to the morgue slab's headstand, the tip of his cane clacking softly on the autopsy-room floor.

"The burking scenario makes preliminary sense, but a few things confuse me," he said. "Take a look."

Robbins motioned toward Rose Demille. She'd been opened up for examination, the scalpel slicing across her collar bone and then down to her pelvis, the flesh peeled back and spread wide. The bony chest plate had been set aside on a work surface near the slab, the heart and lungs placed in hanging weight scales.

For all his dispassion, Robbins had a sensitive hand with the blade. He'd used a T cut on Rose, peeling the flesh upward at her neck in a single flap over her face to reveal the throat structures. The routine Y, with its double incisions up either side of the throat to the ears, left more unsightly stitch lines after it was sewn closed.

"I found froth in her trachea and bronchial canals but nothing lodged in her throat that would block her airway," he said. "And she didn't have any pronounced petechial hemorrhages beyond what I've seen in her eyes. They typically show up as purple rosettes, or spots, above the area of compression on the neck after a manual strangulation, or on the face when violent force is used to stifle breathing through the mouth and nose."

"If she was smothered with a pillow, it would've absorbed some of that force," Warrick said. "Or someone might've covered her head with a plastic bag."

"In those instances, we might not see the sort of trauma that results in petechial bleeding, correct," Robbins said.

Catherine folded her arms across her scrub shirt. "I want to be sure I'm with you here," she said. "You mentioned burking involves pressure to the chest or abdomen . . ."

"Yes," Robbins said. "Possibly even the entire torso. I've seen it in crushing deaths where a person was pinned under a heavy object. A fallen beam, for example. Or a rolled-over vehicle."

"So if you're thinking Rose was burked . . ."

"I noticed faint petechia on her abdomen," Robbins said. "Just a few spots below her rib cage, I could barely make them out. But they indicated a significant weight had pressed down on her diaphragm and made me extremely mindful of internal signs."

"And you found something," Catherine said. It wasn't a question. Robbins had the look of a hunter who'd picked up a trail. She'd seen it in his eyes before.

He turned abruptly from the autopsy table, slipped off his bloody surgical gloves, and tossed them into a pan. Catherine noticed a tiny splatter of red from a glove land on the pan's rim.

Home from school late.

Robbins had reached to lift a wireless remote off a counter and jabbed it at a large wall-mounted flat-screen panel.

"I took a musculoskeletal MRI," he said as the display winked on to show the curve of a spinal column, its vertebrae stacked one atop the other. "Bear with me, I haven't got the hang of this imaging software."

Robbins clicked the remote to enlarge part of the image, clicked again to border it in, then trackballed the arrow cursor onto a blocklike vertebra.

"The twelve thoracic vertebrae are in the middle of the spine," he said. "You're looking at T-11 and T-12. They're in the lower thoracic region, where ligaments, cartilage, and highly movable gliding costovertebral joints connect the spine to the rib cage. The disks are pushed closer together than they should be. And look at the T-11 joint—"

"It's fractured," Catherine said.

Robbins nodded. *Click-click-click.* The CSIs watched the image zoom in another level.

"You see this close-up area? Where it looks like a bit of fabric caught in a zipper?" Robbins moved his cursor. "That's entrapped meniscoid tissue. Soft cartilage pushed between the joint and spinal disk. Similar impingements can be found with two other thoracic joints."

Catherine looked at him. "Was all this caused by whatever left those blood spots under her front ribs?"

"Maybe," Robbins said. "Theoretically, there could be a *range* of causes. Bad posture, a sports injury . . ."

"Bottom line, Doc," Warrick said.

Robbins thought a moment and released a long breath. "Rose Demille was a young woman. If we can believe half of what we read about her, she had a vigorous lifestyle. I doubt she could have gotten through her normal daily activities with a condition this severe—intensive therapy, if not surgery, would have been needed to relieve the acute pain." Another exhalation. "My opinion? These injuries weren't preexisting. She sustained the spinal trauma while being suffocated to death."

Catherine's eyes narrowed. "You said you were confused by something?"

"Mainly, it's that she didn't appear to struggle. Even if she was tied to the bedposts, you'd expect to find some evidence she resisted. Bruising on her hands, arms, or legs, whatever. Assuming she was conscious and alert."

"And assuming she wasn't conscious," Catherine said, "we'd have some indication of what knocked her out."

"Which we don't," Warrick said.

Robbins was nodding. "The negative tox line includes results for common painkillers that might bring on a state of impairedness or incapacitation," he said. "And she didn't take any blows to the head. It's almost as if she willingly, knowingly submitted to being asphyxiated."

He turned off his display, put down the remote, and went to get a fresh set of gloves. The crisp snap as he pulled them over his hands, and the steady pulseless seeping of Rose Demille's bodily fluids, were the only sounds in the unechoing quiet of the room.

Catherine found herself looking at the autopsy table. The first time she'd seen a cadaver opened up, she felt her stomach heave and rushed to lean over a pan. It was the same with most of the other CSIs. Except for Greg, or so she'd heard. Greg being Greg, she didn't doubt it.

The morgue didn't get to Catherine anymore. Here the bloody intrusions fell within a clinical methodology and were done with respect, order, and purpose. But crime scenes were another thing. Crime scenes were the wreckage of rage and madness, and their random violence could still breed horror in her. There was no way to know what to expect at the crime scene. No preparing for it. You entered at your own risk.

Different worlds.

Catherine shook off the thought and glanced at Warrick.

"DNA won't have anything on the hair samples we recovered yet, but Hodges is doing chemical analyses on a strand," she said. "I want to see what sort of progress he's made. Feel like tagging along?"

Warrick checked the time on his wristwatch and grunted. It was almost seven P.M. "I would, but I'm heading out tonight."

Catherine looked at him. "Out where?"

Warrick nodded. "Gonna see what's shaking at Club Random. Where Rose and Mark Baker partied till closing last night."

"How'd you get wind of that?"

Warrick smiled dryly. *"Entertainment 24.* Cable

TV's 'all gossip, all the time,'" he said, and headed toward the door.

"Hey," Sara said, rapping twice on Grissom's open door.

He glanced up from his computer screen. "Hey," he replied.

She leaned her head in. "Can we talk for a minute?"

Why not? Grissom thought.

They exchanged quick, private smiles, and he waved her toward his desk. Grissom normally didn't appreciate having detours to his concentration. But as Sara approached between floor-to-ceiling shelves of specimen jars, he reflected that she was one detour he'd always welcomed, probably going back to when she first audited his lectures back in San Francisco. In those days, however, he'd allowed no concessions to his emotions.

He noticed the sheets of paper in her hands. "What've you got?" he said.

"Catalog pages from an Internet retailer called Mapadi Leather." She sat down at his desk. "It's based in Karachi."

"Pakistan?"

She nodded.

"That's ranging east, all right," Grissom said.

Sara made a slight face. "The outfit manufactures its own goods," she continued, and slid the computer printouts across to him. "It specializes in customized high-end work wear."

Grissom turned the papers around so he could read them side by side. Then he looked up at her. "This is the same sort of pouch belt Green Man had on," he said, tapping one of the pages with a fingertip. "And the identical boots." Tapping the other page. "I recognize the company logo."

Sara watched him, noticing his sharpened interest. "Green Man?" she said.

Grissom shrugged a little. "Blame it on Greg," he said.

Sara glanced briefly down at her lap, pushed a spill of shoulder-length hair behind her ear. Grissom could have pictured the gesture with his eyes closed. It betrayed her amusement—and her shyness.

"As you can see, he wasn't dressed in hiking gear after all," she said. "It's prospector's apparel. Mapadi's boots are made to order."

"Were you able to get its contact info?"

"I left a voice message maybe two hours ago. Then I sent an e-mail requesting a list of their U.S. customers. I explained I was a criminalist with the Las Vegas Police Department, but nobody's responded."

"I'm not surprised. Karachi's across the international dateline. It's only eight in the morning there." He sat thoughtfully tugging his ear, then said, "Come over here. I want you to see something."

She got up, went around, and moved behind his chair. On his computer monitor was a blue-stained image of three short, rod-shaped structures.

"Chromosomes," she said, leaning forward. "What from?"

"The egg cluster we found in Green Man's mouth," Grissom said. "I extracted them, took a digital micrograph, and ran it against my databases of aquatic egg layers."

"And found a match?"

Grissom nodded and clicked his mouse. A CG image of chromosomal rods overlaid the electron-microscope photo, meshing perfectly with it.

"Here we go." He pointed at the words on top of the superimposed images and read aloud. "*Stygobromus lacicolus*. That's a crablike organism."

A few strokes on his keyboard, and another window opened at center screen. It showed a pale, segmented creature with bristled limbs and antennae.

"Our mama crab," Sara said. "She's almost without pigmentation . . . doesn't seem to have any eyes. Is she blind?"

"Blind *and* one of only two species of arthropod to inhabit the caves of Nevada," Grissom said. "These creatures live in complete darkness. And wouldn't survive more than a few hours outside their natural habitat."

"Hours? That's all?"

"Hours at best. They're very fragile. It's one

major reason they're on the EPA's rare and endangered list."

Sara's brow creased as that sank in. "If the crab that laid the eggs wasn't from Fairmark Lake—"

"Green Man would've become host to the eggs in a different body of water before winding up there," Grissom said. "Probably an underground pool."

"And the algae that's all over him? Wouldn't it *need* the sun to grow?"

Grissom nodded. "He most likely picked it up afterward in the lake. At least, that seems a logical sequence . . . unless we've overlooked something."

Sara considered that a moment. They had a man in miner's or prospecting gear. They had eggs deposited in his mouth by a subterranean crab. And what else?

It struck her like a bolt.

Flash flooding, she thought. *Just days ago.*

"Gil," she said. "Do you think this man could've washed into the lake from somewhere up in the hills? Say, a cave or a tunnel?"

Grissom was looking at her over his shoulder.

"That occurred to me," he said. "There was a fair amount of sandy material in his boots. And in what was left of his socks. I'm hoping it can be matched to a unique geological location."

"Is Hodges doing the analysis?"

"Right after he finishes up with hair samples from Catherine and Warrick's asphyxia victim,"

Grissom said. "In fact, Green Man's next in line for a postmortem."

Sara thought a second. "Want me to see if I can goose things along?"

Grissom rose from his seat. "It's the shift supervisor's job to do the goosing around here," he said. "Didn't you know?"

With the evening cool and pleasant, Warrick had decided to get some fresh air and hoof it to Club Random instead of driving there from headquarters. He was strolling briskly west on Sahara Avenue toward the Strip when Catherine buzzed his cell.

"Yup," he said, nearing the corner. "What've you got for me?"

"Oro Adonis," Catherine said.

"What?"

"It's a high-end salon hair-coloring product."

"Oh."

"For men."

"Oh."

Warrick paused at a stoplight as a limo the size of an Arabian caravan turned onto Sahara from Kendale Street, probably leaving the country club. While he waited, a passenger window lowered along the stretch's shiny white length, and a woman in a swoop-necked blouse leaned out to wave at him. She was gone with the flow of traffic before he could even consider waving back.

The signal turned green. Warrick left the corner, halting in midstep to avoid the front of a huge oncoming double-decker bus that had lunged through the changing light.

"Okay," he said into his phone. "I take it the hairs we got off Rose's sheets were treated with this Hora Apollo dye."

"*Oro*," Catherine replied. "That means 'gold' in Spanish. The hora's a traditional Jewish dance they do at weddings and bar mitzvahs."

"Sorry I missed that. I was trying not to get run over by a Deuce bus."

"Okay, then. Anyway, we ran a chemical matrix test on a bottle of the dye. The formula's a point-by-point match with the tint on the hair shaft."

Warrick continued on toward the glow of the downtown hotels and nightspots. This was important news. Very important, in fact, since he'd checked out some of Mark Baker's recent photos on Internet sports and celebrity gossip sites and noticed that he'd taken to streaking his hair.

"Anything else?" he said into the phone.

"There was another strand of dyed blond hair in the gym bag," Catherine said. "It was tucked away in the neck hem of a folded T-shirt. I kept a segment to test for the coloring formula before sending the rest over to the DNA lab."

"Oro Adonis again?"

"Actually," Catherine said, "it's Oro Olympus."

Warrick reached the corner of Santa Rita, glanced both ways, and hustled across. *Gold Olympus?*

"So does this mean the hairs aren't from the same head?" he said.

"I didn't say that. My guess is they are. The dyes both belong to a product line called—"

"Don't tell me. Oro for Men."

Catherine chuckled. "Attaboy," she said. "Warrick, you know those shots of Mark Baker posted online?"

"Either you're reading my mind, or I left my browser window open."

"My secret," Catherine said.

It was Warrick's turn to laugh quietly. "You beat me to the punch—I was gonna ask you to take a close look at those pictures before we finish talking. See anything interesting about them?"

"Baker's had a foil job on his hair."

"A *what*?"

"Foil job. It's when a stylist separates thin sections of hair with a comb, brushes on dye or lightener, and wraps the sections in foil so their colors don't run together," Catherine said. "A foiling's done for subtle effects and can be really expensive at top-notch salons."

"Not that you've got personal experience."

"Some blondes have naturally great highlights."

"I bet," Warrick said. "You check out salons that use the Oro shades?"

"I will tomorrow morning," Catherine said. "It's eight o'clock—past closing."

Warrick grunted as Catherine signed off. The action hadn't even begun to cook where he was headed.

Club Random was a short distance up the Strip, its entrance almost hidden between bigger and bolder hotel façades. Its planners had shot for a discreet, tucked-away feel, cleverly modeling it after an old-fashioned speakeasy, and Warrick thought they'd been successful. Or as successful as could be expected in this busy tourist hive. The gift shop out front sold souvenirs such as photo calendars of early Vegas casinos, Flamingo and Stardust sand globes, repro antique slot machines, and shelves full of other 1940s- and '50s-themed merchandise. As he entered, Warrick saw a burly guy in a plain brown suit hovering toward the rear and a twentyish blonde wearing a sexy gangster costume behind the sales counter.

"Good evening, sir," she said with a beaming smile.

" 'Evening," Warrick said.

The woman came around into the aisle. With her long hair spilling from under her fedora, she sported a tight pin-striped jacket over a tighter pin-striped vest, a white collar and a black bow tie for a nonexistent blouse, a tiny pin-striped skirt, and stiletto heels. Seamed black stockings going up and up her endless legs above the pumps.

"Are you with *Parlé?*" she said.

"No," he said. "That someone's name?"

"Sir?"

"*Parlé*. I was asking if that's a person."

She blinked. "I guess you aren't with *Parlé*."

Warrick looked at her, thinking it would be great to know what the hell she was talking about. He reached into a hip pocket of his jeans, got out his card holder, and displayed his identification through its plastic window.

"My name's Warrick Brown," he said. "Las Vegas Crime Lab."

Her blue eyes went from the ID card to his lean face.

"Sorry," she said. "*Parlé de Tabou* is a new interactive reality show. On FriendAgenda . . . the Web site, you know?"

Warrick nodded. "I've heard of it."

"The show's about adventurous dating relationships," she said, her eyes lingering on his a moment. "With young, sexy people . . ."

"Right."

"When you came in, I thought you might be a cast member. They're having a series launch party tonight."

Warrick cleared his throat, feeling flattered. "I'm here on a police matter," he said.

"Oh," she said. "I am *really* sorry, Officer Brown. I must seem like a total idiot to you."

"Not at all," he said. "And Warrick's fine."

The blonde smiled, gave him her hand to

shake. "My name's Charity Hayes," she said. "Is it anything to do with Rose Demille? The police matter, that is."

Warrick tilted his head curiously. "Yeah," he said. "What makes you ask?"

"The reporters and photographers have been hassling us. When her maid found her body, you know. Leaving one voice message after another, barging in. Just awful." She shook her head. "Half an hour ago, Bobbo had to toss a few out of here."

"Who's—?"

"That'd be me," said the guy in the brown suit from the back of the shop. "You wouldn't believe those fuckin' scumbags."

Warrick gave him a nod and looked back at the blonde.

"Ms. Hayes—"

"Charity, please."

"Charity," he said, "did you see Rose here the night she died?"

The blonde nodded. "No way could you miss them."

"Them?"

"Rose Demille and the Fireball. Mark Baker. It was a private birthday bash for him, did you know?"

Warrick shook his head.

"Even with lots of faces around, they were *the* couple. I heard they were getting married . . ."

Warrick was thoughtful. "Did you notice how

they were acting? Pick up anything odd from their body language?"

"I'm not sure what you mean."

"Just in the way of an impression."

"Not really. Except that they both seemed in up moods. But I try not to keep people out here too long."

"By that you mean . . . ?"

"Make small talk out here in the shop, especially with famous guests. Athletes, movie stars, musicians, they're always stressed over their careers. And they come to let go of everything. My job's just to greet them and show them into the club."

Warrick thought some more. "Charity," he said. "Do you remember if Rose and Baker left together?"

"No. But I went home early—"

"They did," Bobbo said. "I had the door."

Warrick glanced up the aisle at him. "What time would it have been?"

"When they left? I'd guess four, four-thirty Sunday morning," Bobbo said. "We go till sunup on weekends, so that's right around closing."

"And there was nothing odd about them?"

Bobbo shook his head. "Just the opposite. They were lookin' pretty frisky with each other."

Warrick sighed. "Is anybody else here tonight who also worked the birthday party? Bartenders, servers, DJs?"

"Nova," Charity said.

Warrick gave her a questioning glance.

"Nova Stiles," Charity said. "She's a waitress. And she was Rose's best friend, knew her better than anybody in town."

Warrick's eyes narrowed. "I'd like to go back and talk to her," he said.

"Sure," Charity said, and turned toward the rear. "Bobbo, how about bringing him inside?"

The bouncer nodded, stepped over to a picture on the rear wall, and tilted it sideways. The wall slid inward, a wave of multicolored lights and loud dance music pouring into the storefront.

"Nice trick," Warrick said. He smiled at Charity before turning up the aisle.

"I found three discrete crystalline components to the material," David Hodges said, looking pleased to have an audience.

Grissom and Sara swapped doomed glances. This would raise to a multiple of three the amount of surplus information they'd have to hear about the sandy stuff in Green Man's socks and boots. Knowing the lab tech couldn't resist trying to impress people with the full scope of his scientific acumen, they'd clung to the feeble hope that it would have only a single mineral constituent.

"Less than two percent consisted of cookeite," Hodges went on. "That's a triciclinic crystal silicate and a member of the chlorite group. It was named for Josiah Parsons Cooke Junior, a nineteenth-century Harvard mineralogist—"

"Anything exceptional about cookeite?" Grissom said. When had a discussion with Hodges ever concluded smoothly? Grissom couldn't recall one that he hadn't needed to clip off.

"Cookeite's a feldspar, the most common mineral on earth. It's found in both magmatic and metamorphic rock. But the particular crystalline structure of cookeite makes it unique," Hodges said. "The nearest recorded locality I could find for a cookeite deposit is Ramona, California. After that, we'd have to look at Quartz Creek, near Pitkin, Colorado. Then Custer County, South Dakota."

Grissom massaged his chin. "Are you telling us there isn't anyplace in this general area where someone could've stepped in cookeite?"

"I'm telling you I went online and looked for any claims for cookeite mining with the Nevada Bureau of Land Management. I also went into the Division of Minerals database to check for recent permits. Nothing was recorded, but registration easily could be pending. Landowners submit applications all the time."

Sara's eyes touched Grissom's.

"Landowners as in miners," she said.

"Mining firms account for most apps filed with the DCNR," Hodges said. "The law requires that they're prepared by licensed geologists."

Grissom considered that. "Tell me about the other minerals you found," he said after a moment.

"There was a higher amount of another feldspar called microline. It accounted for about ten percent of the material." Hodges perked up, relishing the opportunity to please Grissom. "Microline is a polymorph—it can exist in more than a single crystalline form."

"Is that significant?"

Hodges nodded. "A microline crystal's shape is its morphological fingerprint. If you know what to look for, you can get a picture of the specific conditions that formed it."

"Meaning we can distinguish microline found in one location from deposits in another."

"That's right," Hodges said. "Incidentally, certain microlines are used in costume jewelry. Back in the 1950s, one type that became fashionable in necklaces was—"

"Let's stick to what was on the Green Man's feet." Grissom instantly regretted his unfortunate choice of words. But Hodges seemed oblivious.

"Quartz silicate was the predominant component. That didn't surprise me, since it's the second most common mineral found in the earth's crust behind the feldspars," he said. "The upper crust of the Spring Mountains is largely made up of deposits that fall into those categories."

Grissom turned to face Sara. "The relative percentages of the minerals in Green Man's boots don't tell us much," he said. "Dispersion's going to be random if our sample is only based on where he's stepped."

"And what's to say he picked up all that grit in the same place?"

Grissom nodded. "On the other hand, it *would* help to have a geological map that tells us where the three minerals are found together."

"Especially since cookeite's pretty uncommon."

"Say we collect soil and sand samples from those areas. We can examine the microline they contain . . ."

"And compare them to the microline that came off Green Man," Sara continued. "If any of their crystallization patterns turn out to match it . . ."

"*Then* we'd have something," Grissom finished, and pointed an approving finger at her.

"The closest chapter of the Nevada Mineralogical Society is on the Aldren campus in Reno," Hodges broke in. "After that, it's Winnemucca."

Grissom briefly wondered if Hodges had decided to offer the CSIs a comradely tip out of obligation—after all, the career ladder was a high climb for techs, and who knew when the sometimes misanthropic but always sycophantic Hodges would need somebody's recommendation.

Sara merely grunted, her eyes still on Grissom. Then they turned toward the door together.

"You think it'd be worth my taking a trip down to Reno?" she said as they walked off. "It might be worth talking to a geologist there in person."

"Might be," Grissom said. "Call first. Once you

set something up, I'll fill out a req slip for travel expenses."

"Great, I'll keep you posted."

And with that, they whisked into the hall, leaving Hodges alone in the lab.

The sensory barrage in Club Random's main room was overwhelming. Its large open dance floor thumped with loud electronica, swirled with rainbows of laser light, and was thick with laughter and grinding, closely packed dancers.

Warrick stepped up beside Bobbo as the fake shop wall slid closed behind him.

"Place hops," he said.

Bobbo nodded toward the pole islands across the floor. "You want to see it hop, stick around another hour or two," he said with a grin.

Warrick watched the crowd from within a glittery laser shower. "Where can I find Nova Stiles?" he said, raising his voice above the music.

"The private party's got its own room. She's doin' bottle service."

"How about you point me in the right direction?"

"Do you one better." Bobbo gestured with his chin. "That door off to the side leads to the Hangover Lounge."

"That really its name?"

"It's what I call it."

"Uh-huh."

"Room's quiet, soft chairs. People go there when they need a break from the action."

"Uh-huh."

Bobbo grinned. "You chill in the lounge," he said. "I'll get Nova."

Warrick started around the pumping bodies, felt a tap on his arm from behind, and glanced back. Bobbo hadn't moved except to reach out with a huge hand.

"This's tough for Nova," he said.

Warrick nodded.

"I'm talking about what happened to her friend." Bobbo's hand stayed where he'd put it.

"Right."

"She shouldn't be at work. Leastways serving those Internet shits. But she needs the money," Bobbo said. "I bring her over, you better go easy with your questions."

"Got you," Warrick said.

Bobbo nodded and turned into the crowd.

The Hangover Lounge was subdued as advertised, with very little music seeping through the soundproof walls. It was also empty, maybe because it was still early for the clubgoers to have drunk too much or to realize they'd drunk too much. Warrick found a cushioned chair and waited.

After a few minutes, Bobbo stuck his head into the doorway amid a blast of sound. "She's on her way," he said.

"Thanks."

"Don't forget we got a deal."

"I won't forget, man."

Bobbo left. Warrick waited some more. After a few minutes, Nova Stiles arrived.

She was tall, slender, and leggy, her outfit consisting of a sequined halter top and a low-riding miniskirt, thigh-high fishnet stockings, and glitter pumps. The skirt looked glued on, and strings of beads hung from the halter over about ninety miles of bare, flat midriff. A green feather headpiece made her long red hair look several shades redder.

Warrick sat across from her in the relative quiet of the lounge, reminding himself it was beside the point noticing what a standout she was among the sexy daters at the *Parlé de Tabou* affair now in partial swing outside the room. Even so, if Nova's eyes hadn't been so bleak, he might have found it harder to keep from being distracted by the rest of her. But her carefully applied makeup couldn't hide their puffiness or the dark crescents under them.

"So . . . what do you want to know?" Nova asked.

"Start at the beginning. How did you two meet?"

"Well, I was a receptionist at a spa on South Decatur . . . answering phones, making appointments . . . when she showed up."

"The place have a name?"

"Niki Rusellia's . . . it seems like yesterday."

"How long ago was it really?" Warrick said.

"About six, seven years, I guess," she said, and smiled sadly. "Rosie always turned heads. Gorgeous, maybe five foot nine, killer bod. With that New Orleans belle accent and a style of her own. She drove a midnight blue Porsche . . . a Targa."

"Some car," Warrick said, thinking it had to have cost a hundred thou before they even plunked an engine under its hood.

"You could tell she was used to playing the belle," Nova said. "It was how she carried herself. But she never treated people like they were beneath her."

"And the two of you became friends while you were working there at the spa?"

"From day one," Nova said. "We'd talk whenever she came in. She was new in town, and maybe kind of lonely. And I was going through a rough time. Shacked up with a bad-news guy, needing to get away from him, but not making enough to move anywhere . . . just stuck, you know."

"Yeah," Warrick said. "Think I do."

Nova expelled a long sigh. "She . . . Rosie, that is . . . already had a fancy apartment on Brine. I catch my boyfriend playing around and somehow wind up being the one to regret it. A few days later, I'm at work with a black eye and an Ace bandage on my wrist, when who comes in but Rosie? She gets a load of me and tells me I can stay with her. As long as I need to."

"You accept the offer?"

She nodded. "She practically insisted. I didn't think I could afford my share of the expenses, but she said I shouldn't worry. Whatever I could kick in would be fine."

"How long did you stay on with her?"

"Over a year. She treated me like a sister. Looking back, I think the companionship was good for both of us."

"And why'd you eventually leave?"

Nova started to say something but stopped. Warrick saw her tearing up and handed her a tissue from his pocket. She wouldn't have anywhere to tuck one away in her skimpy outfit.

"Rosie always knew the sort of men that can make things happen," she said, dabbing her eyes. "It wasn't as if she had to chase after them. They tripped over each other to get to *her*. One guy was a partner in a nightclub, the most exclusive place in town for a while. He asks her to hostess, and the first thing she does when she takes the job is put me on her waitstaff."

She dabbed her eyes again. Warrick waited. He could feel the pulse of the dance music outside the lounge.

"Were you working Mark Baker's party Saturday?" he said.

"Yes."

"All night?"

"Yes."

"How'd he seem to be getting along with Rose?"

"You don't think—?" She looked at him. Something had edged up from under the deep sadness in her eyes. "Mark wouldn't have hurt Rosie."

"You're sure?"

"Yes. He loved her."

"I think you know loving and hurting someone aren't always mutually exclusive."

She stared at him another moment, then dipped her head and sat there crying in silence. Warrick could see smudges of mascara on the moist, bunched tissues in her hand.

"Ms. Stiles, this isn't easy, but I need to ask you about a delicate subject," he said. Not that he'd ever found an easy or delicate way to broach it. "Are you aware of Rose experimenting with non-conventional sexual behavior?"

She looked surprised. "What do you mean?"

"Role-playing dramas, that sort of thing?"

"I don't . . . we didn't get into that," she said. "I guess she went for the typical alpha male. Masculine, self-confident, a guy who takes charge when he walks into a room."

"So she never spoke to you about acting out fantasies with her partners?"

"Definitely not. If you'd known Rosie . . . she never talked about her sex life with me."

"Not at all?"

Nova shook her head. "People thought of her as such a free spirit—it sounds weird to say Rose was old-fashioned. In a certain way, it's true, though. She could be very private." She hesitated. "Why do you want to know all this?"

Warrick leaned forward, meshed his hands on his knees. "We haven't made it public yet, but Rose was found tied up and gagged in her bedroom."

Her eyes widened. "My God. I was wondering . . . the news reports said somebody might've broken into her house." She swallowed hard. "How do you know she let herself be . . . that she wasn't forced . . . ?"

"I can't discuss specific evidence. But it looks like she was engaged in a consensual act. At least to a point."

"And you think . . . what? That things got out of control?"

"The best I can say is that Rose being in that situation might've contributed to her death."

Silence again. A young man and woman from the FriendAgenda affair popped into the lounge, got a look at her sniffling with her head down, and about-faced.

Sexy, adventurous, and considerate, Warrick thought.

He rasped his thumb over his beard stubble. "I'd like to get back to Rose's relationship with Mark Baker."

"You think he . . . ?"

"We don't know who was with Rose when she died," Warrick said. "The more information we can pull together, the sooner we'll find out."

Nova sighed heavily but didn't say anything.

"Ms. Stiles—"

"Saturday night . . ." She hesitated, her gaze still lowered. "Rosie told me . . ."

"Told you what?"

She suddenly brought her eyes up to Warrick's face. "A few hours into the party . . . I guess it was a little after midnight . . . she asked to talk. I could tell from the way she came up to me that it was really personal, and I figured this room was the quietest place in the club. So I took my break, and we came in here." She paused, cleared her throat. "We sat here together, and she told me she was getting ready to break it off with Mark."

"Did she give you a reason?" he said.

"Maybe because it started out as one thing for him and then turned into something else," she said. "Rich men like to be seen with beautiful women. Beautiful women like men who can take care of them."

"You're saying Rose dated Mark Baker for his money?"

"Mark took her places. Bought her nice gifts. Sometimes he'd help with her expenses."

"And in return, she made herself available to him."

"I wouldn't put it in those words. You make it sound so cut-and-dried."

"I'm just trying to understand . . ."

"Mark Baker's a star. He can have any woman

you can name hanging on his arm. But he only wanted Rose."

"And what did she want?"

Nova Stiles sat there looking at Warrick, her eyes fiery red from crying. Sat there in her sorrow and loss, a kind of grim resolution slowly forming upon her face.

"Mark was a decent guy, and Rosie had fun with him," she said. "But she was in love with someone else."

Warrick paused. "This someone have a name?"

"I can't . . . I shouldn't say. He's well known. A married man."

"Ms. Stiles, I need to know his name."

Nova hitched in a trembling breath, released it.

"Layton Samuels," she said. "*Dr.* Layton Samuels."

Warrick thought the name sounded very familiar. He prodded his memory.

"The plastic surgeon?" he said after a moment. "The one who's written all those bestsellers?"

"If you're going to fall in love with a guy, it might as well be somebody who can get out the dents and dings," she said with a bleak little smile. And then she started sobbing uncontrollably.

Catherine was waiting for the new coffeemaker to finish its brew cycle when Warrick joined her in the break room.

"Look who's back from Club Random," she announced. "Want a cup?"

He nodded wearily. "Strong and black."

"Here, mine's Italian roast." She lifted her Styrofoam cup from the tray, held it out to him. "You seem to need it more than I do."

Warrick brought the coffee over to one of the cafeteria tables, settled his lean frame into a chair, and sipped. There was a chessboard with several pieces on it a few places down—Grissom was back to his checkmate puzzles.

"So, how'd you do tonight?" Catherine asked.

He filled her in, saw her brow scrunch when he told her about Samuels.

"Isn't he the cosmetic surgeon who's always plugging his books on TV?" she asked.

Warrick nodded. "That's about what I said when I heard his name. Rose didn't mess around with small fry."

Catherine inserted a second coffee pod and pressed the brew button. "Maybe she was preparing for the future," she said.

"Keeping the plastic surgeon close for a wrinkle nine-one-one?"

"Why not? No woman stays young and gorgeous forever."

"Present company excepted, of course."

Catherine smiled. "Of course."

A minute or so passed. The coffee machine hissed and gurgled and served up Catherine's cup.

She sipped, nodded approvingly, and carried it to the table.

"I see Grissom's at it again," she said, sitting down between Warrick and the chessboard.

He grunted. "Probably the Green Man business," he said. "You know he's got a case on mind when he breaks out the board."

Catherine glanced cautiously at the entrance to the room. After a moment, she reached over, slid a white pawn from one square to the next with her fingertip, and then did the same thing with a black pawn.

Warrick looked at her. "What's up with that?" he said.

She grinned slyly. "I've been doing it for years. Gris still hasn't caught on. Can't figure out why his solutions take so long."

Warrick chuckled.

"Let's divvy up our interviews," Catherine said. "You want the famous doc or the sports hero?"

"I'll take the sports hero," Warrick said. "Maybe Fireball'll even autograph one of my baseball cards."

"Why do I suspect you really own one?"

"Maybe I do. It's a collectible from Baker's rookie year," Warrick said. "I told my friends it'd be worth a fortune someday."

"Before or after you snookered it away from one of them?"

Warrick gave her a sideways look. "You up to anything else besides trouble while I mingled with the beautiful people?" he said.

"Listing the names and addresses of the posh-est unisex hair salons in Vegas." She took a sheet of paper out of her blazer pocket. "I have about a dozen we'll need to hit tomorrow . . . check out whether they use Oro products."

"The fun and games never end around here, huh?"

Catherine unfolded the list and glanced over it. "If you ever have a makeover emergency—say, after getting a last-minute invite to a hora party—you'll be glad to find most of them conveniently sprinkled around our splendid downtown area," she said. "In no particular order, there's the Spring Green Spa, the Palmay over at Mandalay Bay, Javanica on West Flamingo . . ."

"Sounds exotic."

"Hmm?"

"Javanica," Warrick said. "The name."

"Uh-huh. I won't forget." She cracked a smile and looked back down at the sheet of paper in her hand. "Okay, let's see . . . we also have the Red Noir Salon, which isn't located on Paradise Road but across from the golf club. Then we've got Niki Rusellia's on South Decatur, Orianna's on—"

"Hold it." Warrick straightened, wound a finger counterclockwise in the air. "Give me the next-to-last one again."

"Niki Ruselli—"

"That's the spa where Rose Demille and Nova Stiles first met each other."

Catherine snapped her eyes up from the list.

"You wondering if Rose might've introduced the Fireball to her chic longtime hairdresser?" she said.

Warrick drained what was left of his coffee.

"Either that, or I'm looking for somewhere I can have my natural Oro-ed out," he said, emphatically smacking the empty cup down on the table.

It was almost midnight before Sara's periodic check of her in box yielded a response from the Pakistani mining supply seller, though its sender was a Y. Sahid at LexInternational.com, rather than the Mapadi address to which she'd sent her e-mail six hours before.

Slouched in front of her computer with a chocolate bar and a cola, she opened the message. It began:

> *Dear CSI Ms. Sara,*
>
> *I am this afternoon in receipt of your inquiry about the leather tool belt and leather boots. These are consisting of two main items in our line of premium quality leather pouch belts, leather boots, leather bags, leather jackets, and other leather mining accessories. As you may know, we are one of the world's leading manufacturers of premium leather pouch belts, leather boots, leather bags, leather . . .*

Sara rubbed the premium leather out of her eyes with her thumb and forefinger, and skipped down a paragraph:

Our understanding is that you wish for the names and addresses of our customers in the United States. Regretfully we must inform you they cannot be provided. It is our policy not to be sharing names and addresses of our customers with third parties.

Your interest in us is appreciated. Please do not hesitate with further inquiries about our premium leather products. You may also register for our free company alerts. Wholesale discounts are offered for large orders.

> *Thank you,*
> *Yassir Sahid, Leather Exports International,*
> *Karachi, Pakistan*

Cursing inventively through her teeth, Sara grabbed the telephone and punched in the international number in the e-mail. After a brief wait, a male voice answered in English.

"Hello, Leather Exports International, how may I assist you?"

She plunged ahead by introducing herself as a member of the LVPD criminalistics unit, explaining that she'd tried contacting the company earlier, and informing him that she was looking at a seemingly irrelevant e-mailed response from someone named Yassir Sahid.

"This is Yassir speaking, Ms. Sara," said the guy at the other end of the line. "I apologize for any previous confusion. May I have your customer reference number, please?"

She frowned. "I don't have one. I'm with the Las Vegas police."

"Yes, thank you. But we will need a customer reference number to review your shipping order."

"I just told you, I don't have a reference number. Or a shipping order. Did you bother reading my e-mail before you answered it?"

"Yes, Ms. Sara. And we sincerely regret the prior difficulties you experienced. So, please . . . do I understand that you have no reference number?"

"That's right. I—"

"Thank you. I am now going to assign you a number. It may be used if you are disconnected or need assistance with this order in the future."

Sara pouched her cheeks and blew out a long stream of air. "Maybe we should start over," she said. "I'm with the police. I haven't placed an order with your company."

"Yes, thank you. But your file must be given a reference number before we proceed, Ms. Sara."

"That's Ms. *Sidle*."

"I'm sorry. Ms. Sidle, yes?"

"Right."

"And for our records, how shall I spell your first and last names?"

"They're already spelled out in my e-mail."

"One moment, please." There was tapping on a keyboard. "I have pulled up your e-mail and can see your full name here, thank you. It is Sara Sidle."

"Right," she said, thinking what a wonderful thing it was to have him confirm it for her.

"That would be first name S-a-r-a . . ."

"Right."

"And second name S-i-d-l-e."

"Right."

"Just another moment . . ." More tapping. "Your correct name is now entered into the system with your reference number. Do you have a pencil and paper so you can write the number down?"

She sighed. "For the last time, I'm calling on police business. And I want to talk to a person who can give me some information."

"Yes, Ms. Sara. But we do have to follow a certain procedure. After you write down your reference number, I will be able to assist . . ."

"Sidle. And I don't—do *not*—want a reference number."

"Excuse me, please?"

Sara closed her eyes, rubbed them again. "Look," she said, "I've asked for a list of people who bought a specific type of tool belt and boots from your company. Either you provide it, or I'm going to call the United States Customs Office and ask that they review your employer's compliance with international trade rules and regulations. Do you understand?"

"Yes."

"Great. And I hope you understand this, too. If they find even a minor—and I mean minor—

trade violation, your boss is going to know it all happened because you refused to cooperate with me over the phone. Is that clear enough?"

"Yes, thank you—"

"Then I suggest you get that information," Sara said. "Right away, thank *you*."

After a brief search through headquarters, Sara found Grissom sitting over his chessboard in the break room, a white pawn in his hand.

"How's it going?" she said from the entryway.

He glanced up at her. "Catherine's been moving my pieces around."

"Again?"

"It's never-ending."

"Why don't you tell her to cut it out?"

Grissom's brows knitted. "Because *then* she'd know I'm on to her," he said, sounding as if that should have been readily apparent.

Sara gave him one of those *I quit* looks, turned toward the snack machine, and inserted a couple of singles into the bill feeder. It dispensed her second Three Musketeers bar of the night along with some jangling coins.

"You remember when candy bars cost less than a buck?" she said, counting her change.

"I remember when people had to pick cocoa beans off trees to make their own bars."

She smiled, sat down beside him, and affectionately rubbed his shirtsleeve.

"I got in touch with Yassir Sahid of Leather

Exports International," she said. "Manufacturer of premium leather pouch belts, leather boots, leather bags, and leather blah, blah, blah."

His face was mildly questioning. "Sounds as if you got an earful."

"An earful, a headache . . . and a list of customers in America who bought belts and boots identical to Green Man's."

"Any of them local?"

Sara pulled a notepad from a pocket of her simple brown blazer and flipped it open. "Last year, a guy named Chuck Belcher with a Barfield mailing address got *two* belts and *three* pairs of the boots," she said. "In fact, he special-ordered one pair in a woman's size."

"Really."

"Yeah. The address doesn't seem currently valid . . . it's in a trailer court," Sara said. "I'll have to call the post office tomorrow and see if there's a forwarding location." She gave him a look. "Want to know what *else* is interesting?"

"Shoot."

"I followed Hodges's lead, scarily enough, and checked the online registry of prospecting claims with the Nevada Department of Minerals."

Grissom's face suddenly lit up. "And you found one under Belcher's name in the database?"

"A beryllium mine filed jointly by Charles and Adam Belcher," she said. "They got their approval two years ago. And the site's right in the Spring Mountains."

Grissom sat quietly staring at the chess piece in his fingers. "Better put in your call to the Mineralogical Society first thing tomorrow morning," he finally said. "If they can lasso an expert mineralogist to consult on short notice, then I'd like you to fly right on down there. Don't worry about a reimbursement; I'll get the expense tab okayed."

Sara poked her tongue against her cheek. "Will that include a car-rental allowance?"

"It's a ten-minute drive from the airport to the university," Grissom said. "The Washoe County sheriff owes me a favor. He'll send a man out to give you a lift."

"Any other budget tips I should bear in mind?"

"Make sure you book an economy flight."

She sighed and took a gooey bite of her candy bar. "Reno, here I come," she said.

"It's not that easy being green . . ."

Nick Stokes entered the morgue room to find Greg standing just inside the doorway. His arms folded across his chest, he was singing in a barely audible undertone as he watched Robbins go about his work.

"What in God's name is going on here?" Nick said in a hushed voice.

Greg glanced over his shoulder at him. "Doc Robbins is taking a CT scan of the Fairmark Lakes floater," he said.

Across the room, the ME had wheeled his mobile computerized tomography unit toward the multitier cold chambers occupying an entire wall of the autopsy room.

"I wasn't talking about the doc," Nick whispered. "I meant, what was that sick croaking noise I heard from you?"

Greg looked at him. "Is this about making me the butt of your good ol' Texas boy humor?"

"No," Nick deadpanned. "I wanted to know about the croaking. So I could help if you were in pain or something."

Greg looked at him some more. "You watch *Sesame Street* when you were a kid?"

"Of course. Everybody watched *Sesame Street* when they were kids."

"Then, you ought to know that Kermit song."

"What're you talking about?"

" 'It's Not Easy Being Green'? The song popped into my head after the floater was dredged out of the lake."

"That so?"

"Right. The reason being that the floater's green. And now I can't get the melody *out* of my head. Or the lyrics. Which is funny, because I didn't even realize they'd stuck with me."

"Life sure is strange, ain't it, bro?"

Greg looked injured but didn't comment. Guardedly optimistic that he was all sung out, Nick looked back across the room at Doc Robbins. He had pulled the floater's body out of the cold case on its stainless-steel rack, then pushed the doughnut-shaped CT tube around its head.

Greg glanced over at him. "You check out the MRI soft-tissue data for Green Man?"

"I've already imported it into Profiler," Nick said. "We're set to go once we add this tomography."

Greg nodded tightly and stood watching Doc Robbins adjust his lead apron over his chest, turn on the machine, and wait as the scanner began to rotate. Ten seconds and a single revolution would produce sixty-four X-ray slices of the dead man's cranium.

Nick turned to him. "C'mon," he said. "Let's get ready to put our model together at my workstation."

"Why not use my computer?"

Nick gave him a long look. "Because mine's in a singing-free zone," he finally said.

The computer application, dubbed Profiler, was a fusion of advanced CT imaging and facial-recognition software. It had been developed to create high-accuracy models of faces that were distorted by crimes and accidents, their soft tissues often eaten, rotted, burned, or stripped down to the chalk-white underlying bone.

As Doc Robbins's scanning apparatus had made a rapid turn around the floater's head, its images were routed to Nick Stokes's workstation via instantaneous wireless transfer. Now Nick opened

Profiler, accessed the fresh-from-the-morgue up-loads, sat back, and watched the program run its gamut of automated iterations.

The first step was a multiplanar reconstruction of the CT slices into a full view of the dead man's skull—his cranial orbit and facial bones detailed down to their foramina, sutures, and processes. Seated in front of the large flat-panel display, Greg and Nick waited as their model took shape, the CT slices stacking up into an image with three-dimensional volume and contours.

The next step excited Greg—a flythrough of the virtual skull's inner and outer features to examine its structural integrity. His hand cupped over a trackball mouse, he navigated his way across the nasal bridge, went in through an eye socket, cruised behind the zygomatic, lachrymal, and sphenoid bones, then flew out the nose cavity to circle the temporal bones and swoop back in between the maxilla and mandible. Going deep into the mouth, its rows of teeth surrounding him like rock formations in an underground cavern, he dove down to the base of the skull, and up again, and finally exited through an auditory meatus.

"Whee," he said. "I'm jazzed."

Nick smiled a little. "Enough fun and games, Rocketman," he said. "Better do our mapping."

A click of Nick's mouse launched Profiler's third-phase synthesis of its facial image. Connecting lines instantly began to form between nodal points on the skull, plotting a grid around the CT reconstruction.

Within seconds, the wire-frame topology was complete.

"Perfectamundo," Greg said. He looked at Nick. "Got Green Man's hard tissues down. Now for our meat and gristle."

He closed the tomographic image file, leaving only the wire-frame on-screen—a proxy skull on which the software would generate its digital face.

Step four was adding the skin and its embedded muscles. Gathered from the MRI scans and computer-adjusted for postmortem deformations, the soft-tissue values were drawn from anatomical and forensic data sets and would be further refined as Profiler built up the facial model. Being dependent on the CSIs' existing knowledge about Green Man's condition—and how he came to that condition—the forensic data had a large number of undetermineds and was the reason their model could never be totally accurate. But they had input enough for the approximation to produce an identifiable likeness.

Or so Greg and Nick hoped.

They watched as the musculodermal bands were pasted onto the wire frame one by one. The masseters. The inner and outer frontalis muscles. The wide ring of the orbicularis oris around the mouth . . .

The fifth and last step was layering on the model's skin surface. Greg stuck to basic Caucasian textural and color elements, then blended in some darker skin tones based on likely tanning. If the guy had been a prospector, as Sara and Grissom believed, it seemed reasonable to assume he'd have been exposed to the sun's effects.

And that was that. Twenty minutes after they'd sat down at the workstation, the CSIs had a photo simulation of a blunt-featured man with large, fleshy cheeks, a thick nose, and a small, round, recessed chin.

Greg studied the printout and scratched behind his ear.

"Dude's mug isn't real handsome," he said. "In fact, I'd honestly have to say he's kinda ugly."

Stokes plucked the photosim from his hand, shaking his head. "I guess it's *not* easy being green," he said.

"Knock, knock," Greg said, standing in Grissom's doorway.

Grissom looked up from his desk, his pen suspended over the requisition form he'd been filling out.

"What is it, Greg?" he said.

Greg came into the office with the Profiler visualization. "Our gnarly friend's no longer a Green Man without a face," he said, passing it across to Grissom. "Courtesy of modern computer technology."

Grissom examined the picture a moment, rubbing his thumb over the cleft in his chin that Sara—oddly, in his opinion—was always finding some reason to compliment.

" 'The worst of faces still is human,' " he said.

"*Sesame Street*?" Greg asked.

Grissom leveled a placid stare at him through his glasses. "Johann Casper Lavater," he replied.

4

SARA SHOT OFF the tarmac at McCarran at one-thirty in the afternoon, landed at Reno-Tahoe about ninety minutes later, and was met by a pleasant and alacritous sheriff's deputy named Vasquez.

"My car's out in short-term parking," he said, nodding his chin at her saddlebag briefcase. "Want me to carry that for you, ma'am?"

Sara smiled. *Ma'am*. Was it her imagination, or did he really look about fourteen years old?

"S'all right, thanks." She started out of the terminal. "It doesn't weigh much of anything."

The Aldren College campus was a brief stint north of the airport on US-395, followed by another on I-80 and then a drive of a maybe a mile on local streets toward the main entrance on Center Street. Vasquez went past the gate in his cruiser, hung two quick rights, and pulled into a meter parking lot.

"We're looking straight at the back of the student union building from here," said the deputy, motioning out the window with his chin. He'd gotten a map of the school out of his glove box and spread it open on his lap. "The Mineral Research Center is just off the old quad." Pointing to a spot on the map. "You'll find the Mineralogical Society offices up on the second floor . . . I called ahead."

Sara slid out the passenger door and declined when he offered to walk her over instead of waiting back in the patrol car.

"See you when I'm done," she said.

"You need anything, call on my cell."

Make that fourteen with a schoolboy crush, she thought, and slung her bag over her shoulder.

She started toward the quad, Vasquez's good-natured attention putting a lift in her step. Though her heart fully belonged to Grissom—atriums, ventricles, blood in, blood out—it was encouraging to know she could draw the tadpole's attention.

The timing was perfect. She'd barely slept, and that had left her muzzy, but campuses were a downer anyway, no denying it. As a student at Harvard and then Berkeley, Sara had relaxed in the classrooms and lecture halls, grown her confidence, felt large and tangible for the first time in her life. But out in the bright open spaces, she meekly faded away, passed among the laughing, hand-holding students like a silhouette or a disembodied ghost. On rare instances, she'd emerged from her introversion and solitude, pushing off self-consciousness, challenging her inhibitions. There was that hazel-eyed and popular guy once—but she had shared little beyond the physical with him and eventually gave up the experiment in disappointment.

Now she crossed to the north side of the quad with a certain insolent poise. If there were still days when the quiet shadows reached out to her, today wouldn't be one of them.

The Mineral Engineering Building, and the connected Mineral Research Center, were modern latecomers among the red-bricked, colonnaded structures bordering the campus lawn. Sara left the grass, took a concrete walkway under a row of graceful elms past the main entrance, and then hooked around the building's south door toward the center out back.

The walls of the Mineralogical Society's reception area were lined with glass cases full of gleaming gemstones and rough mineral samples. Perusing them while she was announced, Sara immediately thought of them as inorganic counterparts to Grissom's floating animal and tissue specimens. Well, sure, she would allow they were more socially palatable. But they made her feel right at home.

Curtis Gaines, the head of the chapter, was

coming around his desk when the receptionist showed her in.

"Ms. Sidle, a pleasure to meet you," he said, his hand extended. "Your trip was all right, I hope?"

"Fine," she said. "I appreciate you seeing me on such short notice, Dr. Gaines."

He motioned her toward a chair in front of his desk and pulled another up alongside it. "Care for something to drink? Soda, water, coffee—"

"Water would be great," she said.

Gaines went across the room to the corner water cooler and opened its refrigerator door.

"Professor Shane Evercroft heads our gemology program—he's on his way over from a class he teaches," he said. "Please make yourself comfortable in the meantime."

They didn't have long to wait. A tall, rangy man in his fifties with sunbaked features and shoulder-length white hair pulled back in a ponytail, Evercroft appeared in the doorway before Sara even took a sip of her water.

"Sorry I'm late," he said after exchanging introductions with her. "Give me a captive audience, and I'll torture a whole lot of ears."

Sara smiled. "Guess you're in luck," she said. "I'm here to listen."

Evercroft sat down in the empty chair beside her. He was wearing a white Oxford shirt, jeans, and glossy western boots.

"So I understand you're trying to identify some

unfortunate person," he said. "What can I do to help?"

Without further preamble, Sara explained how Green Man was found in Fairmark Lake.

"The body was in a decomposed state," she continued, reaching into her case for a manila folder. "I'd like to show you a facial reconstruction we did with a computer-modeling program. And then have you tell me if you recognize this man."

Evercroft took the folder, flipped it open, and drew in a sharp breath.

"Goddamn," he said, studying the Profiler image. He pulled it from the folder and held it up for Gaines to see. "Curtis . . . look at this!"

Gaines's eyes stayed on the picture for ten full seconds before they shot to the professor's.

"I can't believe it," he said in a startled tone. "That's Adam."

Sara jumped right in. "Adam Belcher?"

Evercroft looked at her, nodding his head. "We've known Adam for years. He's a respected gemologist. Self-taught, but as knowledgeable as anyone you'd meet."

"Adam's published articles in some of the field's leading journals," Gaines said. "He's donated literally hundreds of rock and gem specimens to universities and museums around the country."

"Does he have a relative named Charles?"

"That's his brother, Charlie," Gaines said. "Is he okay?"

"I don't know," Sara said. "We haven't got much to go on as far as what's happened."

Evercroft snapped his head around toward Sara. "Do you think foul play was involved?"

"We think it's possible," Sara said. "Again, we don't know a whole lot. Other than that it looks as if Adam's body was transported to the lake from a different location."

Evercroft raised his eyebrows. "What location?"

"I was sort of hoping you could help with that part," she said, and paused. "Before I forget, do either of you know anything about Adam and Charlie having staked a joint prospecting claim?"

"Yes. They've done extensive gemstone mining throughout the state," Evercroft said. "Mostly as a team, I suppose. Why do you ask?"

Sara didn't answer that. There were certain things she didn't want to disclose. Not just at that moment. "Adam had mining clothes on when he was found," she said instead. "There were mineral traces in his shoes and pants cuffs . . . the type of sandy material you'd pick up while you were doing an excavation. Or maybe scouting out sites."

"You know its composition?"

"Cookeite, microline, and quartz silicate," she said. "They ring any bells?"

Evercroft and Gaines exchanged glances.

Sara raised her eyebrows. "Gentlemen?"

"The brothers have a quarry up in the mountains," Gaines said. "Not too far from the Blue Diamond wash."

"Over Red Rock Canyon?"

"Right. Near the public lands."

"Any idea what they've been digging for?"

"Yes," Evercroft said without hesitation. "Beryl."

Ah, Sara thought. She'd never heard the name of a stone sound so loaded with implication.

"Tell me something," she said. "Are the particles from Adam Belcher's shoes the sort you'd find around beryl deposits?"

Evercroft gave the computer likeness of Belcher another glance and replaced it in the folder.

"They're likely components of the matrix," he replied. "You need to understand that beryl can take on different appearances and properties. Depends what other elements are intercalated into the crystals—made part of them on formation. Green beryl's familiar to most people as emerald. We consider them precious gems because they're kind of rare and we like how they look in earrings and necklaces. But red beryl, or bixbite, is a hell of a lot rarer and more valuable. On the other hand, aquamarine, or blue beryl, is a semi-precious stone. And colorless beryl—goshenite—isn't worth much except to costume jewelers who buy it wholesale." He paused. "Though some people want to call it pink emerald nowadays, pink beryl's known as morganite to old-time gem fanciers. After J. P. Morgan."

Sara was curious. "You mean the financier?"

"One and the same," Evercroft said, folding his arms across his chest. "Back around the turn of the last century, Morgan was a famous customer of a fella named George Frederick Kunz, who was the top gem expert for Tiffany's. Far as rarity goes, pink beryl falls somewhere between the red and blue varieties. But call it whatever you want, collectors go at it tooth and nail over an exceptional specimen."

"And that's the type of beryl Adam and Charlie have been mining out in Red Rock?"

Evercroft produced a long exhalation. "What they were mostly finding at the site was clear beryl and maybe a little gem-quality aquamarine," he finally said. "Then they hit a pocket with some morganite. Most crystals are sort of pale . . . I suppose you'd say they're a peach color. They were all the craze a while back, but the color's unstable. Leave the stones anywhere there's sunlight, and they'll fade out to an almost opaque pastel. But the deposit Adam and Charlie hit on was deep pink—the highest gem quality. Those crystals don't fall out of fashion. They fetch the highest market value year in and year out."

"Sounds like the brothers really scored," Sara said.

"I think it's fair to call that an understatement," Gaines said, and then looked at Evercroft. "We ought to explain just what a singular find it was, Shane."

Evercroft continued, thoughtfully. "Twenty years ago, a Maine quarry came up with the largest deep pink morganites ever discovered in North

America. It was thirty centimeters wide across the basal pinacoid—the two faces of the base. Once word of the find got out, everybody wanted to get their hands on it. Museums, schools like ours, private enthusiasts . . . it turned into a whole damned war. In the end, the miners that owned the morganite got tired of being stuck in the cross fire and had it cut into smaller gemstones—a tragic decision if you happen to be a gem lover."

Sara digested that for a second or two. "Are you saying the Belchers unearthed a stone as good as the one from Maine?"

"Better," Evercroft said. "Theirs was a richer color and a full forty centimeters wide."

Sara looked at him. "That's more than a *foot.*"

"Trust me," Evercroft said, "it's an unbelievable specimen. I've seen it with my own eyes."

"And where is it now?"

Evercroft sighed. "I don't know," he said. "When Adam announced the discovery in a journal about six months back, the fireworks between competing interests got started again. This time, it turned into a family feud, though. The Smithsonian wanted to put it on display and made an offer Adam was inclined to accept. But I heard that Charlie insisted they auction it off to collectors, figuring they could draw a handsomer profit that way. Gloria . . . I'm not sure where she stood."

Sara was puzzled. "Who's Gloria?"

"Gloria Belcher, their mother," Evercroft said. He spread his hands. "An unpleasant woman. She put up at least some of the money for their beryl dig. Or that's what I think. I'm not sure they could have financed it on their own. Or even agreed on a partnership."

"Why's that?"

"The brothers are complete opposites," Gaines offered. "Adam's easygoing and friendly. I've always enjoyed talking to him." He hesitated. "Let's say Charlie takes after Gloria and isn't too well liked."

Sara stared out the window behind Gaines, remaining silent as she watched the students sunning themselves down on the quad. Then she looked alternately at Gaines and Evercroft.

"Do either of you remember when you last saw Adam? Or his brother?"

Evercroft shook his head. "I'd guess a month for Adam. Maybe a little longer . . . he was here at a Society function, isn't that right, Curtis?" he said.

"Yes. He came alone," Gaines said. "As for Charlie, I can't even remember the last time he showed his face."

Sara sighed, thought a moment, turned to Evercroft. "Is there any more information you can give me about their mining projects?" she said. "Their latest one in particular?"

He gave her a wan smile. "Absolutely. Though it's possible you'd find everything I can tell you on the Internet. And gallery photos of the morganite to boot."

She tilted her head. "Any tips on where I'd look?"

"It's customary to name an outstanding gemstone after it's registered," Evercroft said. "The Patricia emerald, the Mandalay ruby, the Star of Bombay, American Star diamond . . ." He let the sentence trail. "To see how famous the Belchers' stone has already gotten, you just need to Google its name."

"That being?"

Evercroft uncrossed his arms. He still had that thin, sober smile on his face. "Sorry, I thought I already told you," he said. "It's called the Nevada Rose. Catchy, don't you think?"

Mark Baker was staring west toward the mountains from the shade of a bristlecone pine when he heard the veranda's screen door swing open and shut behind him, followed by the sound of footsteps on the sunbaked tiles.

"How are you?"

"Fine." He did not turn around.

"No, you aren't."

"Why bother asking if you're that sure?"

"Maybe so you'll share what you're going through."

"Everything's okay. I can handle this."

"Sitting out here alone for hours on end . . . that's what you call handling it?"

"It's waiting, is what it is. And thinking. I can't do much more that's useful until they show up."

"What makes you certain they're—?"

"We can't close our eyes to reality. They'll show before long. I have to prepare myself. Decide what I'm going to tell them."

"There's the truth."

"The whole truth, and nothing but the truth . . ."

"Please, don't make it sound like I'm naïve. You know I'm doing my best to help."

"I know. I'm sorry."

"These secrets . . . I'd keep them forever if you insisted. But I don't want to see them be the end of you. That's too high a price."

"They could be the end of me no matter how I cut it. If that's the case, I've got to choose which ending's easiest to stomach."

"And aren't I worthy of a vote?"

"Worthy, yes."

"I don't get one, though. Do I?"

He still had not turned from the hills. Once upon a time, he thought, fortune seekers had been lured into them by rumors of silver and gold.

"I . . . you . . . no. It isn't fair, but no, you don't. I'm sorry."

"I can't believe it. This is twice already."

"What's twice?"

"That you've apologized. How often have I tried wringing an 'I'm sorry' out of you and gotten pissed because you won't relent? Now I get two for the price of one."

"If you insist, I can take them back."

"My God, was that an attempt at humor?"

"Actually . . . yeah."

"Then I suppose there might be hope yet. Except I want you to do me a favor."

"What's that?"

"Save your apologies for when they're owed."

"And you don't think they are now?"

"No. Not to me."

"And what about Rose?"

"Don't punish yourself. It won't help her or anybody else."

"Unless I'm to blame."

"You shouldn't say that. Not even in private."

"Why? It hasn't occurred to you I might be? Even for a split second? Remember, we're all about the truth here."

"I love you. I could never love someone who had done those things."

Which wasn't really an answer to his question.

Baker resumed his silence. After a few moments, he heard the veranda door open and shut again. He still did not turn around.

The sun, moving down over the hills, jabbed through the branches of the old desert pine, splintering the protective shade around him.

He stared off into the distance, not thinking as he'd claimed but honestly waiting, his eyes those of a man who had come out there to watch his own funeral.

The office of Dr. Layton Samuels, listed in the phone directory as the *Mesa Trinity Cosmetic Sur-*

gery Center and Anti-aging Spa, was in Seven
Hills, a development named after the seven hills
of Rome, even though the architectural motif of
its sprawling, stuccoed, tile-roofed multimillion-
dollar mansions had been chiefly inspired by the
countrified villas of Tuscany, a region of Italy
about two hundred miles from *la città dei sette colli*
as the crow flies, go figure.

This strained, not to say pretentious, nomen-
clatural conceit aside—"What's good enough
for the Romans is good enough for Las Vegans!"
honked the real-estate brochures—Seven Hills
could honestly boast of being among the chicest
of the chicy-chic village communities that had
sprung up in crisp, clear, picture-window view of
the Strip some ten miles northward and the rug-
gedly striking Black Mountain range a like distance off to the south.

As Catherine Willows nosed her car past the
video surveillance cameras to either side of the
center's high iron entry gate, drove on between
parallel lines of dignified palmetto palms, and finally swung under a small grove of peach trees
to halt in the circular front drive, she was thinking this would be a nice, cozy place to come if she
ever decided to have any part of herself enlarged,
reduced, lifted, tightened, tucked, peeled, im-
planted, Botoxed, collagenized, micropigmented,
or otherwise reshaped or redone—medical pro-
cedures she was certain were explained at length
in Dr. Samuels's *New York Times* bestsellers.

Although, after having witnessed autopsies by the score, not to mention far too many grisly hack jobs at murder scenes, she'd seen enough slicing and carving of human flesh to make her singularly uninterested in elective surgery. If she went under the knife, it would be for some damned good reason.

Ding dong.

An attractive middle-aged blonde answered the door almost at once. Catherine thought the woman looked familiar, though she couldn't make up her mind why.

"Ms. Willows?" Smiling. "Please come in. I'm Eleanor Samuels."

Catherine nodded, offered her hand. *Mystery solved.* She'd seen some of Eleanor's talk-show appearances with her husband.

"I appreciate the doctor agreeing to talk to me," she said. "I know I didn't give him much notice."

Eleanor motioned her into the entry hall.

"Your call seemed quite urgent," she said. "I assume this visit concerns a patient?"

Catherine displayed her most effortlessly professional *I can neither confirm nor deny it* smile and then followed Samuels's wife into the foyer. As she went deeper inside, passing from the first hallway to a waiting room and then into a second hall, she tried her best not to look overly impressed by the enormous plasma screens along the walls, each of them gliding through a preprogrammed slide show of pricey-looking artwork.

"They're all from my husband's personal collection," Eleanor said. "Monet, Gauguin, Degas . . . people don't realize Layton holds a Cambridge degree in art history. He's of the conviction that it's influenced his approach to aesthetic bodywork."

Catherine figured it probably couldn't hurt, though she had to believe that any connection between fat sucking and an Impressionistic painting of daffodils might be just a little bit of a stretch.

Mrs. Samuels made another turn, stopped at a wood-paneled door, and reached for the knob.

"This is Layton's office," she said.

Catherine nodded. She'd already read the plaque beside the door.

"Can I do anything else for you?" Eleanor lingered between Catherine and the entryway. "Help with information? I'm very hands-on, running the practice."

Catherine shook her head. "If I think of something, I'll let you know."

Samuels's wife stood there another moment, smiled briefly, nodded. "Please feel free," she said, finally moving aside.

Catherine went through the door into a small anteroom and immediately noticed a painting hung above an antique chair to her right. No plasma image this time, but honest-to-goodness oil on canvas.

"It's from Picasso's Blue Period."

She spun around toward the sound of the voice, almost bumping into the man who'd come up to stand behind her—presumably Layton Samuels. Standing about six feet tall and weighing a fit hundred and eighty pounds or so, the doctor had a horseshoe fringe of gray hair around his otherwise bald pate and a short, neatly clipped beard. He wore a black T-shirt under an eggshell blazer, with charcoal slacks and loafers. Catherine guessed he was in his late fifties.

"Dr. Samuels," she said, "I'm—"

"My wife told me you'd arrived, Captain Willows."

Catherine raised an eyebrow as they shook hands. Unless she'd missed something, Eleanor hadn't announced her.

Samuels must have seen the question on her face.

"Our security cameras picked you up at the gate," he said. "And then at the front door. Since I canceled all appointments for the afternoon, we just assumed you were our visitor."

Catherine nodded at the explanation. She was about to suggest they sit down to talk, when Samuels motioned toward the painting on the wall.

"Beautiful, isn't it? It's the crown jewel of my collection."

Catherine turned to regard the oil again. Rendered in monochromatic shades of blue, it showed two women in robes and shawls standing together near an archway, one with her head bowed penitently, the other seeming to offer her stern consolation.

"Very beautiful," she said. "Sad, too." And valuable. High-ticket plastic surgery certainly did pay.

"The Blue Period started with a close friend's suicide and lasted about four years," Samuels said. "This was done after Picasso visited Saint Lazare, a French women's prison. The inmates were prostitutes, most of them with venereal diseases, and their guards were nuns. It must have been hoped the sisters would steer them toward absolution."

"Better late than never," Catherine said, and looked at him. As he continued admiring his pride and joy, it occurred to her that Samuels did not seem like a man having anything that resembled a blue period over his lover's death. Or like someone who was even aware of it. But Rose Demille's apparent murder was making front-page headlines. Unless Rose's friend Nova Stiles was wrong about her relationship with the doctor, that seemed peculiar, to put it mildly.

Samuels studied Catherine's face a moment before he motioned her toward the door to his inner office.

The room had black leather chairs along the walls, a sleekly abstract bronze of a female nude in one corner, and a huge quarter-sawn oak desk as its focal point. Catherine sat down at the desk, giving Samuels a chance to settle in on the other side.

"I didn't mean to talk endlessly about my art out there," he said, angling his head in the general direction of the anteroom. "Give me any time away from my patients, and I forget myself."

"That's all right," Catherine said. "It isn't every day I get the chance to stand around admiring a Picasso."

Samuels smiled. "My wife says you some questions for me," he said. "Eleanor says that when she spoke to you on the phone, you didn't mention what they might be."

Catherine took a deep breath. "Dr. Samuels, I'm here about Rose Demille."

He gave her a vague look. "What do you mean?"

Catherine was used to that being the obligatory first response. She couldn't recall a single married person she'd ever questioned who'd admitted an affair without prodding. Not that she necessarily thought Samuels was faking his confusion.

"As you may be aware, she died several nights ago under mysterious circumstances," she said. "There's an ongoing police investigation to try to determine what happened."

Samuels nodded, rocked forward in his chair. "I heard what happened to her. Like everyone else in Vegas. The story's all over the news. But why are you talking to me about it?"

"I have information that you were having an intimate relationship with her," Catherine said. "Is this true?"

He shook his head. "I'm a happily married man, Captain Willows."

Which Catherine was very aware was neither a yes nor a no. Again, not saying she was prepared to tag the doc's answer as evasive. She sighed heavily. "Are you telling me you didn't know Rose Demille?"

"That isn't what I said."

"Then could you please help me understand what you *did* say?"

"We'd met. I don't know where this information of yours originated, but there's no scandal to the story. She came here once or twice quite a few months ago."

"By here, you mean—"

"The center," he said. "She wanted to consult about possibly having a cosmetic procedure."

"And what happened?"

"Nothing." Samuels made a small gesture with his hands. "She elected to pass on the work. Or possibly chose to get it done elsewhere. I wouldn't know."

"Can you tell me what sort of work it was?"

Samuels shook his head. "I don't recall. This *was* a while back."

"But you'd have a record of the consultation?"

"It really depends on how long ago it was. My wife's proficient with computers and handles that end of things. I think Eleanor keeps old appointments archived in the office scheduler for several years, so there might be a date and a time. But in this case, she wouldn't have bothered leaving a notation about the reason for her visit."

"Because?"

"If there's no follow-up with me, it becomes irrelevant."

Catherine thought a bit. "And that's it? There was no further contact between you and Rose Demille?"

Samuels rocked back and forth in his chair some more, hesitating.

"Doctor . . ."

"I'm not sure," he said. "We may have had a casual conversation or two at some point."

Catherine looked at him, suddenly cognizant of his rocking. It might mean he was nervous, but that wasn't necessarily significant. Most people got nervous when somebody with the LVPD came around asking questions. And it might also just mean he liked to rock when he talked.

In any event, right now, she was more interested in the meaning of his last response.

"I don't follow," she said. "Did you or didn't you see Rose after her visit?"

Samuels shook his head. "I lead a very public life," he said. "Las Vegas is a small town in many ways. We occasionally mixed in the same circles, were invited to the same parties . . . I remember that we did bump into each other at some social function or other. But I couldn't tell you when that might've been. Or if it was before or after the consultation. Whatever we talked about, I know it wouldn't have been anything but chitchat."

Catherine watched his eyes. "Dr. Samuels, can

you think of any reason someone would lie to the police about you and Rose Demille being involved in an affair?"

"I wish I could," he said. "As it is, I have no idea who's accused me—"

"I wouldn't call it that."

"What?"

"An accusation," Catherine said. "People tell us things for different reasons. I don't think anyone was pointing fingers."

Samuels's chair creaked. "Be that as it may," he said, "I can only repeat that I'm very identifiable to the public. I don't want to sound like a broken record. Or like I forget to count my blessings. But there are downsides to everything. When it comes to being well known, one of them is that you're left open to all sorts of talk."

"And you're stating that you and Rose Demille weren't romantically connected?"

Samuels leaned forward again. He closed his eyes a moment and rubbed the bridge of his nose with his thumb and forefinger.

"Captain Willows, I don't expect you to tell me exactly what happened to that unfortunate young woman," he said. Opening his eyes now to look straight into Catherine's. "From the stories leaking out to the press, I suspect it may be something monstrous and can only hope she didn't suffer for a foolish mistake."

Catherine looked back at him. She was thinking that once she was through with the doctor here, she would have to hurry up and find out what the hell kind of stories he was talking about.

"Mistake?"

Samuels expelled a long sigh. "Rose Demille was unapologetic about her way of life," he said. "To answer your question . . . my practice may help people shape their outward appearances, but its success comes from them trusting who I am inside. That I'm the man I represent myself to be in books and on television. I could never jeopardize everything I've built up—my marriage, my public reputation—with some thoughtless extramarital fling." He paused, sighed again. "One thing I've learned is that secrets have a way of baring themselves."

Catherine met his gaze with her own, shrugged.

"Some do, Doctor," she said. "But from my own experience, there are others that seem to need a helping hand."

The first thing Warrick noticed outside Niki Rusellia's was the owner's massive face next to the lettering on the salon's logo. What struck him as he entered a moment later was that none of the staff members was working. Not to say they *hadn't* been busy before he came in— everything Warrick saw told him they must have been in a full groove. The place was thick with the unmistakable salon smells of perm solution, peroxide, and perfumy shampoo. There were male and female clients with aprons thrown over them at mirrored hairstyling stations. There were clients with their heads tilted back over sinks, their hair sudsy and dripping wet. There were clients under the dryers, at the waxing and manicure booths, and waiting in chairs at one side of the door.

But the fact remained that Warrick Brown had found the entire crew of the chichi salon standing motionless at their respective stations with their scissors, sprays, brushes, blow dryers, color tubes, and assorted other hairdresser's whatnots in hand, as if they were playing freeze tag or had maybe swallowed some weird, immobilizing magic potion.

A moment later, he realized that every single person in the salon—clients, staffers, everyone without exception—had his or her eyes trained on a big wall television over the waiting area.

And *then* he abruptly understood what had gotten their attention.

At an anchor desk on-screen were a man and a woman Warrick recognized as two of the rotating hosts for the Entertainment 24 cable gossip network. The woman was a perky blonde with large hoop earrings and a retro-style bob. The metro male beside her had swirled, thickly gelled hair and a pasted-on white strip of a smile. The graphic behind them, a huge photo of Nevada Rose Demille in a black low-necked dress, was captioned: "*ET/24* Headline Story: Police Suspect Murder in Nevada Rose Sex Death."

"I can't hear anything," said a female stylist to Warrick's right. "Somebody turn up the sound."

An elaborately manicured redhead behind the reception desk pointed the remote at the set and turned it up.

Warrick stood inside the salon's doorway, stock-still like everyone else, his eyes glued to the TV screen.

"In a stunning revelation about the death of thirty-four-year-old Nevada Rose Demille at her home early this week, Entertainment 24 *has confirmed that authorities are now theorizing it may be related to sadomasochistic sex,"* said the woman in hoop earrings, the camera moving in for a tight close-up. She paused, approximated a sober journalistic face, and turned to her cohost. *"Lorne?"*

"Thanks, Koko," he said, replacing her on the screen. *"As the investigation into Nevada Rose's tragic demise heats up, so have police made her allegedly hot sexual escapades a target of intense scrutiny. As part of our ET/24 exclusive, we've learned that evidence allegedly discovered on or near the grounds of Rose Demille's fashionable Mariah Valley residence has led the LVPD to zero in on Rose's rumored fiancé, baseball legend Mark 'Fireball' Baker, as a possible suspect in what could be developing into a homicide investigation."*

Another pause, and it was back to Koko.

"A short while ago, ET/24 *celebrity crime beat correspondent Roxxii Silver tracked down the case's lead*

detective, Captain Jim Brass, outside police headquarters. He had these comments in response to her questions . . ."

Warrick watched as a video clip of Brass appeared on the set, noticing he wasn't actually outside the departmental HQ but was getting out of his car in the crime lab's parking lot. Of course, *ET/24* wasn't exactly acclaimed for the accuracy of its coverage.

"Captain Brass, what can you tell us about reports of Rose Demille participating in bizarre sex games with her alleged killer?"

This had been Roxxii, speaking off camera as the lens zoomed onto Brass's bulldog face.

"We've got nothing for you at this time," Brass grunted. Surprise, surprise.

"Would you at least comment on stories that Rose's home was filled with what have been described as 'erotic lingerie' and 'kinky paraphernalia'? And that an item, even possibly a murder weapon, belonging to a prominent sports figure has been retrieved from outside the—?"

"I repeat, we've got nothing for you." Brass again, the picture of him wobbling crazily as he pushed past the cameraman.

Warrick smiled a little. He could have warned Roxxii.

The broadcast cut back to Koko in the studio.

"Well, Lorne, that was enlightening." Rolling her eyes.

"Par for the course, Koko," he said. *"But ET/24's*

viewers can be sure we'll be on top of this unfolding story in coming days and weeks." He sighed, his expression lightening. "*Next up after a commercial break, our feature story on the paparazzi and pop diva moms. How far is too far when—?*"

The television suddenly blinked off, the salon returning to life a moment later. Warrick turned toward the reception desk, saw a thin guy with an ostrich crest of spiky black hair holding the remote, and recognized his face as the same one above the salon's entrance.

He went up to him, flashed his ID. "Mister Rusellia—"

"Those ghouls make me sick," the stylist interrupted. He nodded at the screen and lowered his voice. "Shitbags are dancing on Rose's grave."

Warrick looked at him. "I need to ask you a few questions," he said.

"Listen, I don't know anything about what happened to Rose the other night."

Warrick looked at him some more. "Her boyfriend a client of yours?"

"Rose had a lot of boyfriends."

"I think you know the guy I mean," Warrick said. "If you'd be more comfortable talking somewhere else—"

Rusellia held up his hand and stepped closer. Warrick saw his eyes flick up to the crown of his black departmental baseball cap.

"Cee-Ess-Eye," Russelia said, reading the letters off the front. "What's that stand for, anyway?"

Warrick wondered why he hadn't asked when he saw the badge. But whatever got him to open up, he thought with a mental shrug. "Crime Scene Investigation," he said.

Rusellia looked satisfied. "Baker's a client," he said in a confidential tone. "I do the work on him myself."

"How long's he been coming here?"

"Four, five months. Rose referred him."

"And the last time you did his hair?"

"Maybe two weeks ago."

"A foil job."

"You got it, man."

"What products you use?"

"Strictly Oro for Men. Numbers twelve and sixteen. That's Adonis and Olympus."

Warrick looked at him. "Okay, thanks."

"That's it?"

"For now."

Rusellia went back to staring at the top of his head.

"There anything else you want to know about my cap?" Warrick said.

"No," Rusellia said. "Not about the cap."

"Then what?"

"Your hair."

"My *hair*?"

"Right. It getting thin or something?"

"No."

"You sure? Because I got a special formula of my own, treats hair loss." Rusellia winked at him.

"This way, you can stop hiding it underneath these caps."

Warrick reached for the cap's brim and flipped it off to display his thatch of coarse reddish-brown hair.

"See?" he said. "No thinning."

Rusellia eyed his head a moment and winked again. "That's some rockin' natural," he said.

5

THE NEW ADDRESS Sara had gotten for Charlie Belcher from Evercroft and Gaines was outside town in a place called the Sunderland Trailer Court.

She drove out with Grissom just hours after returning from Reno, and as he swung right off Route 612 onto one of its branching two-laners, it became apparent that this forlorn neighborhood around twenty miles from the Strip might easily have been a whole wide world away.

In the heart of Sin City, the flooding had been little more than a passing, unsightly inconvenience. Better drainage had mitigated the effects of the heavy rains, and its worst eyesore transgressions had been cleaned up within a week or two. Lane closures for road repairs were brief and smoothly coordinated. The government had turned its manpower loose where it counted—in the gaudy tourist playground where people who didn't live within a thousand miles of Vegas spent their cash.

But travelers did not flock to the city for snapshots of low-income residences with clotheslines hung outside and three-wheeled beaters on concrete blocks in the carports and tumbled plastic kids' toys in the beaten patches of grass and dirt out front. Where there was no inflow of tourist dollars to counter the waters that had furiously come raging down from the mountains, many roads were still without restored banks, and some remained collapsed in places where the rushing torrent had washed out the drainage culverts that ran beneath them. If the damage wasn't too extensive for patchwork fixes, local firefighters and county cops had rigged temporary repairs out of wood planks and truckloads of gravel to allow passage. Other lengths of road were simply barricaded off with yellow traffic cones and an occasional deputy routing vehicles onto negotiable detours.

Looking out her window as Grissom bumped along in fits and starts, Sara saw few NDT bulldozers and heavy-duty trucks around and had a feeling the sheriff's men would be out waving drivers onto hastily improvised bypasses for a long while to come.

She unenthusiastically sipped the lukewarm

coffee they'd picked up at a local filling station, swished it in her mouth, gulped, and pushed the cup into the holder.

"I think that's the access road up ahead on the left," she said, pointing.

Grissom drove on for another quarter-mile and then swung off the main road.

The court had been hit hard by the flood, and its residents were still sorting through the wreckage it left behind. Charcoal grills, cheap lawn chairs, and plastic lawn furniture were toppled everywhere. A little girl's pink dollhouse lay splattered in mud like a weird play version of the horrendous mess her parents must be dealing with. As she continued to look out her lowered window, Sara could smell mold and mildew from the water damage inside the trailers.

"Charlie Belcher's in Unit Twenty-four," she said.

Grissom glanced back and forth out the windshield. "Which way's that?"

Sara checked her map printout. "A right, a left, and then another sharp left," she said. "It should be near the end of the road."

Parked on a small lot right where the satellite map said it would be, Unit 24 was an aged, white, rust-scabbed Skyline Nomad double-wide with do-it-yourself painted blue shutters and a transportable front deck nailed together out of weathered gray wood. Grissom pulled the car to a halt four or five yards away from the trailer and then sat looking at it for a minute.

"Charles Belcher looks to be down on his luck even by Sunderland Trailer Court standards," he said with a thin smile. "I suppose it just goes to prove treasure hunting isn't as romantic as it's cracked up to be."

Sara slipped on her sunglasses. "Do we really need proof?" she said. "Evercroft told me the brothers were making out okay for quite some time. But they put themselves in hock to lease and finance their latest mining project."

"The morganite dig?"

"That's right."

"And finding the Nevada Rose led to a falling out between them."

"I'm not clear on how it ought to be characterized," she replied. "I know Adam was supposed to be the purist. He wanted to accept the Smithsonian's offer because the museum could guarantee the Nevada Rose wouldn't be cut up for jewelry. He was afraid a private collector might do it even if he said he wouldn't, or that it'd be resold to another collector or dealer who would, or that whoever bought it would take good care of it for a decade or three and then die and leave it to an heir who'd cut it up."

Grissom considered that. "Commendable," he said.

"You're thinking you'd feel the same about your bees."

"And my specimens," Grissom said. He smiled

faintly again. "Fortunately, I know someone who'll be a good steward if something happens to me."

Sara glared at him through her dark glasses. "When it comes to that formaldehyde pig fetus, don't count your luck," she said, and reached for her door handle.

Before she'd even swung her legs out of the car, the trailer door opened, and a woman stepped onto the weather-beaten deck boards.

Thick, wavy gray hair flowing past her shoulders, she was a big woman—as tall as Sara but a good fifty pounds heavier. Probably around sixty, she wore a loose-fitting men's T-shirt, a plain brown prairie skirt, and large, inexpensive-looking red-framed glasses. She had a wide, homely face, and it appeared she did not bother with makeup.

Sara pushed the rest of the way off her seat, Grissom emerging from his door at the same moment. She remembered Evercroft and Gaines telling her Charlie Belcher lived with his girlfriend and that his mother was staying either with him or with Adam in a separate mobile unit at the court. Sara also knew the brothers were both in their thirties, giving her a fair hunch this was the mother.

She tried to recall her name. Jodie? No. Jacqueline? Though it was written in her notepad, she didn't open it there in front of the woman. People always got nervous and put off when they saw someone from the police bring out a pad, and she already looked wound up enough.

She came out to the splintery edge of the deck, her hands clenched at her sides, moving with a slight hitch in her step.

"You're here about my son," she said. Her voice shaking, hands closing more tightly. "I know you're here about Adam."

Sara looked at her. She read more than anxiety in her tone and body language—there was a kind of angry aggression, too. This wasn't anything unusual. When you came to deliver bad news, it was human nature for the recipient to blame the messenger. And when you as the messenger wanted someone to stay calm, it started with being able to call that person by his or her name.

Sara tried to get her memory to cooperate. What *was* this woman's name? Jolene? Not that either, no. But almost . . .

Ah, okay.

"Gloria Belcher?" she said. "I'm Sara Sidle with the LVPD. And—"

"Tell me what happened to my baby boy!" the woman shouted. She shook her fists, her eyes flaring white behind the outsized frames. "You goddamn better tell me where he is right *now*."

Sara took a deep breath.

So much for calm, she thought.

The hardest part of the job for Grissom was notifying someone of a loved one's death. Walking up to a door, knocking or ringing the bell, waiting for the door to open with the weight of a mountain on his shoulders. And then looking into the face of the husband, the wife, the mother as he broke the news.

Grissom was a contained, analytical man, rarely given to open displays of emotion. But it would have been a mistake to conclude that he lacked empathy simply because he was not demonstrative of his feelings.

If certain times were worse than others, none was easy. Like anyone else, Grissom related differently to different people. His reasons might be quantifiable, intangible, or a combination of elements. Did the face at the door remind him of someone he knew? Was the victim a child? A teenager? An elderly man or woman? How had he or she perished? By what means?

Grissom's center of gravity rested around scientific investigation. Knowing the cause and circumstances of death were necessary for him, and realizing what its agonies must have been came along with that knowledge. There were instances when he could place himself fully and completely in the skin of a victim, rewind to the last hours and minutes of life, and then track forward through the series of events leading up to the final painful blow or wound, the gasping struggles for breath as the body's systems shut down.

At the age of seven, he'd begun collecting

animal cadavers from the beach for autopsy. He was ten when his grandmother died. The day it happened, he had stood outside his mother's bedroom door and overheard her phoning close friends and family members. Grandmother had suffered a massive stroke, his mother tearfully explained. The doctors had said it stemmed from a brain aneurysm.

Stroke? Grissom, seeking to understand this new term, had read through his encyclopedia, studied its medical and anatomical diagrams. Then, stifling tears of his own, he had ridden his bike out to the canals near the beach and pedaled up and down their concrete walks for hours, scouring the plant growth and sand along the water. Finding a dead raccoon in the shrubs, he brought the furry remains home for autopsy and opened the animal's skull. As he cut into its brain, Grissom deliberately punctured one intracerebral artery with the tip of his scalpel and observed the cold blood flowing out onto the table.

When he was finished, Grissom had thought he'd understood what killed his grandmother. He had hoped, as well, to understand better the cause of his inner ache. But he was less successful in that.

At church for the funeral service, Grissom had turned his eyes toward his grandmother's casket and kept them there. Staring at the flower sprays and wreaths that bedecked its lid, he imagined the sudden hemorrhage from a burst artery in Grandmother's brain, pictured its lobes and whorls swamped in blood.

Seeing Grissom bow his head while he took communion at the rail, Father Donnelly had laid a hand on his shoulder and offered a few quiet words of solace.

He'd been mistaken. Finding what he'd learned from his autopsy a shield against his terrible sense of helplessness, the boy had wished to thank the dead raccoon for giving him what an unseen God could not. By contrast, the father's sermon, and the hymns sung from the pews, had made Grissom feel lost and untethered.

But that was long ago. The laboratory was Grissom's only church now, its test tubes and Bunsen burners his phials and censers. Possibly whatever followed death was like the biblical metaphors of sleep and eternal peace. Possibly it was, but he did not spend much time thinking about it. Where was the evidence? The data? Without facts, he would never know.

What Grissom did know and understand were the physical processes that began when a killer's hand shot out of the shadows. He knew the route this shocking visual stimulus would take to the ventral and dorsal streams of the victim's cerebral cortex. He knew how the alarm reaction pumped adrenal hormones into the blood, knew the mechanism by which the hippocampus and amygdala went into throes of growing panic, knew the neural pathways by which the pain of being shot or stabbed reached the somatosystem. Grissom knew these things and much more about dying and death, and his mind would draw graphic perceptual parallels as he contemplated how a life must have ended. At times, he almost felt torn from his body, as if he were having a lucid nightmare or his consciousness had been projected into another self.

Grissom still wasn't quite sure how Adam Belcher had met his particular end and had not even conclusively determined that the body in Robbins's morgue belonged to him. While that seemed highly probable based on the mining gear Green Man was wearing—and Gaines's and Evercroft's unequivocal recognition of the Profiler image—the CSIs had neither established what killed him nor decided how he'd wound up floating in lake water. Furthermore, it would be a broad and irresponsible jump to start speculating about fratricide based solely on what Sara was told about Adam and Charlie's relationship.

All Grissom knew, in fact, was that he was about to inform a mother that her son was likely dead. And that she was standing outside her other son's trailer looking very agitated . . . and intensely belligerent in spite of Sara's attempts to settle her down.

This was going to be among the tougher ones.

He stepped forward and announced himself,

thinking he'd better do something to keep the situation under control.

"Mrs. Belcher, it might be best if we speak inside," he said. "I—"

The trailer door swung open again, a man coming out onto the deck this time. Tall and broadly built, with heavy features, brown hair, and a bushy mustache, he had on a pair of bald-at-the-knees dungarees, a checkered shirt with ragged cutoff sleeves, and work boots. Grissom took only an instant to notice his resemblance to Adam—or the Profiler image of Adam. Then he realized his boots were identical to those found on Green Man.

"Charlie Belcher?" he said.

A cautious expression on his face, the man nodded, looking from Grissom to Sara and then back at Grissom.

"You two with the police?" he said.

Gloria's hand shot up before Grissom could answer.

"They are," she said, half turning to Charlie. "And I still ain't heard either of 'em say why they came to see us."

Grissom stood there for a long moment. "What I have to say may be difficult, ma'am. For both of you. I really would suggest we discuss this in—"

"I told you out here's fine." Her voice was trembling again. "You go ahead an' talk, we gonna see where it leads."

Grissom took a deep breath. He was not inclined to inform them about Adam while they were all standing out in front of the trailer. But Gloria wasn't giving him any choice.

He groped for some alternative he hadn't considered, came up blank, and finally gave a slow, acquiescent nod of his head.

"We believe we've found Adam's body," he said. "I'm going to ask at least one of you to come down to see it and help with a positive identification, but we've brought a photograph—"

"You goin' to tell us he's dead?" She scowled at Grissom. "That what you want us to believe?"

He hesitated a second. "We've found the remains of somebody fitting his description," Grissom said. "He was recovered from Fairmark Lake."

"The man-made one?" Charlie said. "Out on that big new golf course in the foothills?"

Grissom kept his eyes on him. "He was wearing the same type of boots you've got on," he said. "From that Pakistani company . . . Mapadi."

Charlie shook his head. "No," he said. "This has got to be a mistake. We ain't the only people around that wear those boots."

"It turns out you are, actually," Sara said, moving up alongside Grissom. "That's how we were able to start tracking you down."

Charlie looked at her and continued to shake

his head, the muscles of his jaw working. "I'm tellin' you," he said. "You got to have made a mistake."

Sara reached into her shoulder bag, produced the file folder she'd brought to show the men in Reno, and held it out to him.

"I have the photo," she said. "We need you to take a look at it."

Charlie remained motionless for a span of perhaps ten seconds. Then he gave a reluctant shrug, came down off the deck, took the folder from her, and looked inside.

"Christ in heaven," he said, studying the computer print. "His eyes . . . they're shut, but he don't look dead." He looked at Grissom. "A minute ago, you told us he was dead."

"The picture's a reconstruction based on MRI and CAT scans . . . he'd been in the water for a period of time," Grissom said. Then, as gently as possible, "Charlie, is this man your brother?"

Belcher stared at him but said nothing.

"Is it Adam?" Grissom urged.

Belcher cleared his throat. "Yeah," he said, nodding. He seemed to sag physically, his hands lowering the open folder from his chest. "Yeah, it's Adam."

"Bullshit!"

Grissom spun around toward the deck. Standing there on its edge, Gloria had shouted out in a cracked, excited voice, her cheeks having at once paled and broken out into splotches of feverish color.

"I don't know what kind of picture you have, but it *ain't* my baby!" she cried, shaking the tight balls of her fists again.

Grissom stood looking at her, Charlie turning to do the same now, his gaze momentarily clinging to his mother's.

"It's him," he said. "It's his face."

"No!"

Gloria suddenly tore off her eyeglasses and threw them off the deck, an outburst Grissom took as a fit of anger, protest, denial, or perhaps all three. Then she doubled over, heaving with sobs. Charlie glanced over at her, pushed the folder back into Sara's hands, and hurried back to her side.

"We're all she's got in the world, " he said, putting his arms around her. "Adam and me."

Grissom nodded. "I understand," he said. Then waited a beat. "Charlie . . . we need to ask, do you have any idea what might have happened to your brother?"

"No," he said. "None."

"When was he last in contact with you?"

"Been a couple weeks since we heard from him."

"Was it before or after the rainstorm?"

"I guess it was right around that time."

"And you haven't notified anyone?"

"No," Charlie said. His Adam's apple went up and down. "He's done it before. Took off without lettin' anybody know where he's gone, that is."

"For this long?"

"Sometimes longer." Charlie paused. "We were havin' a disagreement."

"About the Nevada Rose?" Sara said, stepping up closer to the deck. "I heard you had some friction over it."

Charlie raised his eyebrows, looking almost startled. "Who told you?"

Sara merely shrugged and regarded him through her sunglasses. "We've talked to a few people," she said.

Which, Grissom thought, was a neat way of giving a truthful answer without revealing exactly how much they knew or whom they'd spoken to.

He waited beside Sara. Belcher, meanwhile, stood with Gloria weeping into his chest.

"We had separate ideas about what to do with our find," he said after a moment. "I don't suppose it's a secret."

Sara looked confused. "You and Adam are in the middle of trying to hash out what to do with the crystal, and then one day he just doesn't come home," she said. "What did you suppose he was doing?"

"I didn't know," Charlie said. He was shaking his head. "Guess I figured he wanted to set off on his own and think things out."

"And it didn't occur to you to check? Just to be on the safe side?"

Charlie shook his head again. "You got to know Adam," he said. "You knew him, you'd understand."

"But he was missing for *two weeks*."

Charlie shook his head mutely. After a moment, Grissom gave Sara a look that signaled he wanted to lower the temperature.

"I think Miss Sidle was just asking whether you were at all concerned about Adam. If it occurred to you at any point that he might have gone up to the mine and gotten in trouble."

Charlie was starting to answer when Gloria lifted her head from his chest.

"My son already told you," she said, swiping aggressively at her tears as she tore free of her son's embrace.

"Told us?"

"We wasn't worried about it," she said. "Not at first."

Grissom narrowed his eyes. "Forgive me, Mrs. Belcher . . . but how could you not be?" he said. "Four people are officially known to have died in the flood. And the total hasn't stopped climbing."

Gloria dragged a hand across her eyes again, then stood squinting a little as she looked down from the deck. Grissom thought about the glasses she'd thrown off her face, lying in the dirt near his feet now.

"My boys ain't fools," she said. "Adam knew

about the storm warnin'. I don't care what he meant to work out in his head . . . he been prospectin' since he was sixteen, seventeen years old. With that weather near, there's no way he'd go up onto the slopes without tellin' one or the other of us."

Grissom spent a few moments trying to decide what to make of her insistence. Then he shifted his attention to Charlie. "Have you been to the quarry since the rain?"

"Maybe three, four days ago," Belcher said. "I might've gone up sooner, but the road's been closed."

"And you saw nothing to make you think Adam was there."

Charlie shook his head. "I looked everywhere around our camp. Just to be sure, you know."

Grissom thought some more. "Can either of you tell us if Adam had any enemies?" he said.

His sudden change of tacks visibly upset Gloria—and revived her antagonism. She gave Grissom a hard look.

"Why you come to me with that crazy talk? Askin' that kind of question?" she said. "People like Adam. Respect him. Nobody would want to do him harm."

"You're sure?" This from Sara in a coolly assertive tone. "Because our questions aren't crazy, Mrs. Belcher. We came because your son is dead, and we think there's a fair to good chance he was murdered."

Gloria shook her head with a kind of livid, defiant anger, her cheeks blotchy and tear-streaked, her gray hair flying wildly around her shoulders.

"Don't you talk that garbage here. Don't you *dare* try 'n' tell me somebody killed my son!"

Grissom shot Sara a quick look. He was thinking they would have to back off before Gloria's volatility led her into a total meltdown.

First, though, he needed something from Charlie. He turned in his direction. "If you don't mind," Grissom said, "I'd like your permission to inspect the mining site."

"It wouldn't do us no good," Charlie shot back. "I told you, I looked everyplace for some sign of Adam."

"We have experienced people who may be able to pick up clues you missed," Grissom countered.

"No," Charlie said. "You wouldn't find any more 'n I did."

Grissom's calm blue eyes betrayed no hint that he was suddenly positive Charlie was hiding something important up there at the quarry. "I don't see what's to lose," he said.

Charlie looked at him, opened his mouth as if to speak, and seemed to change his mind. Grissom's eyes didn't waver from his face.

"Though we prefer it wouldn't be necessary to go this route, my lab can obtain a court order to gain access to the camp," Grissom said, keeping his tone level and nonconfrontational.

"Get away from here," Gloria snapped. "You got no business with us."

Grissom slowly transferred his gaze to her. "Ma'am—"

Gloria cut him short with a sharp, hissing expulsion of breath through her front teeth. Then she took a shuffling step toward her son, grabbed his arm, and tugged him back toward the trailer.

Charlie Belcher stayed where he was on the deck long enough for Grissom to pick up Gloria's eyeglasses and hold them out to him. Taking them from Grissom's hand, he nodded and went inside with his mother.

Grissom watched the trailer door shut behind them, looked at Sara, and nodded toward their car. A minute later, the CSIs drove off the way they'd come.

Turning from the access road onto Route 612, Grissom kept one hand on the wheel and reached for his cell phone with the other.

"You calling Brass?" Sara said.

"We need a warrant to search that mining camp," he said.

Sara thought quietly. "Interesting that the Belchers didn't want us to take a look," she said.

"Very." Grissom thumbed to the phone's address book and scrolled down to the captain's name. "I don't want them getting up there before us."

"You think they have something to tidy up?"

"Could be."

They jolted on over the pits and ruts of the flood-damaged local road.

"Guess I'd better fish my nonpremium leather hiking boots out of the closet," Sara said.

Grissom looked across the seat at her. "Let's be ready to set out tomorrow morning," he said, and pressed the call button on his phone.

6

THE MOVEMENT AWAKENED him. Or he supposed it was the movement when his thoughts snapped together. It was the jostling, the slight creak of bedsprings, the bounce of the mattress. He was a naturally light sleeper, although the medications sometimes put him out deep.

Startled, he lifted his head off the pillow. His door was partially open—he wasn't sure whether or not he'd left it that way—and he could see her face close to his in the light spilling through from the hallway.

Suddenly, he wasn't alone.

His eyes widened. She had gotten into his bed, slipped under the blanket with him.

"What are you doing here?" he said. "How did you get in?"

A soft laugh. "Those are some kinds of questions to be asking me," she said. "I used my key, to answer the second one. As for the first, that depends a little on you."

He suddenly wondered what time it was, glanced at the glowing face of his clock, and saw that it was almost two in the morning. Goddamn it, he should have changed the locks. Every last one of them. The complicated inconveniences aside.

"Look, I think you'd better leave," he said. "This is crazy . . ."

"Crazy that we're in bed together? I can remember when we looked forward to it. The more often, the better."

He saw her face above him in the dark. This really was insanity. He couldn't control where it would lead, and that was dangerous.

"You're remembering, aren't you?" she said. Moving closer to him under the blanket. "I didn't think you could forget in such a short time."

She slid against him, and he realized she was naked.

"This is a mistake," he said.

"Maybe."

"It's a mistake."

"If so, we've made worse. Much worse. And managed to live with our regrets." She put her lips close to his ear, tickled his ear with them. *" 'Still in my heart's a sorrow, I'd thought that time would fade, guess it's the kind of love you give, the kind of love we've made.' "*

"Where did you—?"

"I heard you listening to the stereo."

"You . . . when?"

"It doesn't make a difference. I heard." She shrugged her bare shoulders, and sang in a quiet voice. " *'A love of pain and pleasure, a love that lasts forever . . .*"

"Stop."

She laughed. "Why? Is my voice that awful?"

"You're taunting me."

"No, you're wrong," she said. "I'm trying to understand finally . . . and give you what you want."

He felt his pulse quicken. It was what she'd said. The way she had said it. He couldn't deny it excited him. Yet at the same time, there was a kind of angry loathing—for her, for himself.

Neither feeling was unfamiliar.

He felt her naked body press against him.

"I don't know what you're doing," he said.

"I think you do, but it isn't just up to me." Her hand moved over his, guided it to her lips, then down. "There. Go ahead. Show me what you want."

"No . . ."

"Show me."

He turned fully onto his side, pressed his fingers into the soft swell of her flesh, and moved the other hand to her throat.

"You never . . ."

"I do now," she said. "Show me how to be what you want."

He pressed harder with the one hand, squeezed her throat with the other, trying to imagine that it was Rose beside him under the blanket. To imagine the swell of her body, its nearness, its warmth . . . its life . . .

He stopped.

"What is it?" she said.

"Nothing."

"Something's wrong."

"No," he lied. But something was. He couldn't picture Rose. Try as he did, he could not see her in his mind. "I . . ."

"What?"

"Rose," he said huskily. "Rose."

Knowing how that would cut into the woman in bed with him now. Knowing how it would hurt.

Wanting to hurt her.

But she'd asked what he wanted, and he had told her.

He groaned then, his stomach tightening as he rolled on top of her.

"Go ahead," she said. Digging her nails into him. "Go ahead, you son of a bitch, *don't you stop.*"

His rage sustaining him, he didn't.

Warrick could have spotted Mark Baker any-where. The strong jaw, the broad shoulders and slab-muscled arms, the erect, confident posture. A man of colossal stature in size, reputation, and athletic prowess, Mark Baker was the kind of imposing, instantly recognizable figure who would dominate his surroundings wherever he might be. In fact, even his deep, masculine voice was an unmistakable signature as it carried across the sunbathed green at the Las Vegas Country Club, where at any given moment, mega-wealthy residents of the club's gated mansions could look out their windows to see famous personalities honing their golf strokes in their very backyards . . . and where Baker's slick, high-priced lawyer, Vince Millar, had finally, *finally* agreed to let him talk to Warrick about Rose Demille after several arduous haggling sessions on the phone.

"Mr. Brown," Baker said. He took one hand from around his putting iron and extended it. "Glad we could meet."

Warrick nodded in acknowledgment as they shook. He was glad Baker said he was glad, since it would go a long way toward making things go smoothly between them. He was, however, not quite persuaded that his gladness was at all for real, considering that Millar—who was standing alongside his client on the closely mown grass— had argued against allowing their get-together until Warrick angrily threatened his client with a subpoena.

"What happened to that young woman is a

frightful tragedy," Millar said. "I sincerely hope we can be of help to you."

Warrick gave him a nod similar to the one he'd given Baker. The shyster claiming he now wanted to cooperate with the investigation might have been cause to be doubly glad, except Warrick did not think for an instant that his declaration was *remotely* truthful.

"As I told you over the phone, Rose Demille's unexpected passing has left Mark devastated," Millar went on. "I hesitated to have him speak with you prematurely . . . in my opinion, he ought to take more time to recover. But while we've all seen the grit Fireball displays on the field, it's a testament to his makeup that he over-ruled me and insisted on—"

"Thanks, Dave, I think he hears you." Baker had placed a large hand on the attorney's back to interrupt him and steer him aside. "I can speak for myself."

Warrick looked at the former ballplayer. His expansive chest filling out a lemon yellow La-coste shirt, Baker wore a white golf visor over his short, spiky, and very subtly blond-highlighted hair.

"If you don't mind my asking," Baker said, "could you tell me what is it you do?"

Warrick shook his head a little. "Do?"

"At your crime lab," Baker said. His eyes firm. "I'd guess you have people with different kinds of know-how."

Warrick was silent a moment. He'd watched Baker pitch dozens, if not hundreds, of times on television and had seen the same sharpshooter's gaze that was right now trained on him sizing up batters at the plate, evaluating their stances, measuring their confidence, almost seeming to dissect every swing before it was taken. It might have been his imagination that those eyes were looking at him in that same way, but he really felt as if they were, and it was an odd thing. They commanded a force that was intense and tangible.

"My specialization is audiovisual analysis," Warrick said. "But we all pick up a little of this and that."

Baker nodded, half leaning on his golf club. "Happens when you stick around the game long enough," he said.

Warrick was quiet again. Baker looked at him steadily in the sun, the bright golden sunshine adding luster to his blond-streaked hair. Sunbeams struck the bright red flag flapping gently on its stick above the hole.

"The reason I'm out here today's a charity tournament," Baker said. "People bid on getting invited and going a few rounds with me. Been doing it since my third year in the majors . . . makes it my twelfth year."

Warrick glanced past Baker at the fluttering red banner. Written across it were the words "The

Fireball Baker Make-a-Pitch for Needy Kids Invitational."

"This time, we raised over three hundred thousand dollars," Baker said. He'd noticed Warrick checking out the flag. "A hundred percent of it goes to the charity, and I'm as serious about my commitment as I am about anything in the world. But if it wasn't that the bidders already paid their money, I would've canceled." He halted a moment, swallowed thickly. "If that doesn't tell you where I'm at, nothing will. I can't believe Rose is gone. It just feels like a bad dream to me. And I didn't want to talk about it with you or anybody else."

Warrick nodded. An actor he recognized from a cable TV drama about mafiosi with family problems came walking by in golf clothes, his caddie carrying his bag. He paused to lay a fond hand on Baker's shoulder.

"How're you doin', Fireball?" he said with an interested look past him at Warrick.

"All right." Baker gave him a thumbs up. "Glad you could come, man."

The actor smiled. "You asked, I'm here," he said. "See you for lunch?"

"You bet."

The actor squeezed his shoulder, gave Warrick another brief glance, and moved off across the course.

Warrick waited till he was out of earshot. "I'll try to make this quick," he said.

"My client would appreciate that." Millar had stepped forward. "Mark will be teeing off at the tournament's opening ceremony in less than an hour."

Warrick shot the attorney a look of annoyance. He had not thought he'd given the impression he was talking to him. After a moment, he turned back to Fireball.

"Mr. Baker, what was your relationship with Rose Demille?"

"She was my partner."

"And by that you mean . . ."

"We were best friends, lovers, soul mates, whatever words you want to use."

"The press has called you her fiancé. Would you say that's accurate?"

"We talked about getting married. But it wasn't like they reported it."

"How so?"

"There wasn't a definite plan. We were happy with the way things were between us and didn't want to rush."

"Can you tell me what happened the last time you and Rose were together?" Warrick asked.

Baker looked at him. Warrick deliberately tried to act oblivious toward Millar, who he knew would be looking at him, too.

"I have trouble talking about it," Baker said. He cleared his throat. "It isn't any other night."

Warrick nodded again. "That was the case, I wouldn't be here with you right now," he said.

Baker grunted. "No, I guess you wouldn't," he said, and then expelled a tidal breath. "You might know my birthday was a couple days before. But I was in New York to talk about a promotional deal, and Rose said we ought to go out and have a good time when I got back."

"Which of you suggested going to Club Random?"

"She did," Baker said. "But it wasn't like I could've picked a better place. We'd been there a couple times since it opened, and I figured it would be fun." He gave a doleful smile. "What I didn't know was that Rose and some of my buddies were setting me up for a surprise party."

"And when did the party start?"

"I must have picked Rose up at nine o'clock. Got there half an hour or so later."

"You took your car?"

"Right."

"What kind's that?"

"I was driving my Jag," Baker said. "A black XJ."

Warrick nodded. "Anything you feel I should know about what went on at the club?"

Baker hesitated a moment. "I'm not sure," he said. "That is, I don't think there's much that could help you. We were all just hitting the dance floor, laughing, having a good time."

"Could Rose have gone off with someone you didn't know at any point?"

Baker seemed a bit confused. "Gone off?"

"To have a conversation, anything like that?" Warrick said. "Even for a few minutes?"

"I doubt it. We had a private hall, drink service, our own disk jockey." He shook his head. "I guess she might've left once or twice to see a friend who works at the place."

"Nova Stiles?"

Baker nodded. "Nova, yeah," he said. "You've met her?"

Warrick noticed that Baker and Millar were both looking at him.

"I spoke with some members of the club's staff," he said, keeping his response deliberately noncommittal.

Baker nodded. He fiddled absently with his putter, holding the grip with one hand and the head with the other, rotating its shaft across his body. "Once Rose's friend, always her friend," he said. "I think the two of them used to be roommates or something. They stayed close afterward."

"You don't sound like you socialized much with Nova."

Baker shook his head. "We don't have much in common . . . she's from a different time in Rose's life," he said without further elaboration. "Anyway, they might've talked for a while in one of the lounges."

"Do you remember when this was?"

"I'd say around halfway through the party."

"And that would've been . . . ?"

"Around twelve, one o'clock, I suppose."

Which was consistent with Nova's account, Warrick thought.

"After she got back to you," he said, "can you remember if anything about Rose's behavior changed?"

Another head shake from Baker. "No," he said. "She acted the same all night."

"And how was that?"

"Just upbeat . . . that's the best I can put it." Baker toyed with his club. "We were enjoying our friends' company."

"And what time did the party end?"

"I can't say," Baker said. "Wasn't watching the clock."

"Can you take a rough guess?"

"It was pretty late. Or early, depending how you look at it. Rose even joked about how the staff would leave before our crowd thinned out," Baker said. "Don't hold my feet to the fire, but I'd say it was four, five in the morning."

Which jived with the bouncer's recollection, Warrick thought.

He mentally reviewed everything Baker had told him thus far. "So you and Rose leave the club around daybreak," he said. "What happens next?"

Baker seemed about to reply when Millar once again thrust himself partially between them.

"That's about enough!" he said. "Mr. Brown,

you *do* understand my client is trying to prepare for an important charitable event."

"Yes, I do," Warrick said. "We should be through here in a minute."

"I sincerely hope so," Millar said. "Mark volunteered to answer a few brief questions. If you'd advised that you planned a full-scale interrogation in this setting, I'd never have sanctioned—"

"Vince, it's okay." Baker released one end of his putter and chopped a hand in the air, the muscles of his upper arm bulging against his shirtsleeve. "This is about Rose. Not me. And I want to do anything I can for her. Whatever it might be." He turned to Warrick. "Your question was . . . ?"

"About what you and Rose did after leaving Club Random," Warrick said.

Baker was looking straight at him again. "There isn't much to talk about," he said. "I drove her home, then left."

"You didn't stop in at all?"

Baker shook his head. "I needed to get some sleep. My personal trainer comes over for a session every Sunday morning."

"So you dropped her off, said good night, drove away."

"Right," Baker said. "I waited outside the place in my car till she was through her door."

Warrick gave him a puzzled glance. Besides

thinking about the hairs found *inside* the place—hairs found on Rose's body and bed, in fact—that just so happened to look a whole lot like those on Baker's head, he was reflecting that if he'd had the chance to spend his birthday night with a gorgeous woman like Nevada Rose Demille, he wouldn't only be hoping for plenty of exercise right there with her but might very well tell his personal trainer to wait until his *next* birthday until he pried himself away.

If he'd had a personal trainer, that was.

"Something wrong?" Baker said.

"Not really," Warrick said. "I'm just wondering why you couldn't call to postpone the workout."

Baker shrugged as if the answer should have been obvious to him. "I might have if I'd known about the party ahead of time," he said. "But like I told you, it was a surprise. I didn't realize I'd forgot to call Kyle till I was halfway to Rose's house."

"Kyle?" Warrick didn't think he'd caught the name before.

Baker paused a beat. "Right," he said. "My trainer."

"Can you give me his full name?"

Baker kept looking at him. "Kyle Gibbons," he finally said.

Warrick took a pad out of his pocket, flipped it open, scribbled a note inside. "Do you have a phone number for him?"

That suddenly propelled Millar between him

and Baker again. "Okay, that's it, conversation over," he said.

Warrick stood with his pen and pad in hand. "I only had one or two more questions."

"Then they'll have to wait for a more appropriate juncture," Millar said. "I fail to see how Mark's trainer is relevant here."

Warrick did not answer.

"What's going on?" Millar said. "I know the gossip press has been throwing Mark's name around as if he's a criminal, but since when are people tried on television? No one in the LVPD's told me they suspect him of anything."

Warrick still did not answer.

Millar shot darting glances left and right to make sure no one had wandered near the three of them.

"I asked you what the hell is going on," he said in a lowered voice.

Baker stood half a step behind the attorney. "Vince, listen," he said. "I don't mind talking to him—"

Millar shook his head. "No," he said. "I won't allow it. Not until Mr. Brown responds to my question."

Warrick sighed, figuring he'd might as well be up-front. "A gym bag was found on the lawn outside Rose Demille's house," he said. "It had your client's name tag on it."

Baker was shaking his head. "No, that can't be," he said. "Not if it was—"

"Say another word, Mark, and you'll have to find another lawyer to represent you," Millar interrupted. He glared at Warrick. "What sort of disgraceful ambush is this?"

Warrick ignored the comment. He did not want to get into a game of back-and-forth recriminations.

"There's more besides the bag," he said. "Transfer evidence was recovered at the scene. We're going to request that Mr. Baker come into our lab for a medical exam."

"And if he chooses not to?"

"We get a subpoena."

Millar continued to stare. He was openly incensed over what had been sprung on his client, and Warrick wasn't altogether sure he blamed him.

"Mark agreed to speak with you today because he wants to assist in finding whoever killed his lover. He hadn't the slightest feeling you intended to conduct a surprise attack," he said. "You'll need to issue a court order before we comply with any further requests."

Warrick took a deep inhalation. "That the bottom line?" he asked.

"No."

This was from Baker, his huge frame looming over both Warrick and the attorney.

They faced him at once.

Millar said, "Mark, I have to warn you—"

Baker silenced him with an adamant shake of

his head. "Vince, you want to take a walk, I won't stop you. But there's some things I have to decide for myself," he said. Then he once again turned his intense, coolly assaying gaze on the CSI. "I told you how I felt about Rose. And I wasn't lying."

"I didn't call anyone a liar," Warrick said.

"No . . . no, you didn't." Baker hesitated, his lips suddenly dry. "I lost one of my gym bags about a month back and thought I might have left it at Rose's house. But when she couldn't turn it up, I figured I must have misplaced the bag somewhere else and afterward forgot all about it."

Warrick thought about that. "You're sure about when you lost it."

"Yeah," Baker said. "Positive."

"Then how does it wind up on the lawn?" Warrick said. "It doesn't make sense that nobody would've found it in all this time."

"Your guess is as good as mine," Baker said. His voice had become a hoarse rasp. "The same goes for my wanting to know what really happened . . . and *not* to some damned gym bag." He paused, swallowed. "All I care about's finding out what happened to Rose. I suppose there might've been an old boyfriend who had some kind of grudge, I don't know. She never pretended she didn't have a history. But I'll do anything I can for her. Give you whatever you need."

Warrick saw Millar frown with consternation

at being overruled and once again couldn't knock him for it. He'd have done the same if their positions had been reversed . . . making him very glad they had not been.

"I'd consider taking that physical without getting a judge involved, Mr. Baker," he said. "The better we're able to evaluate the evidence, the faster we can clear things up."

"Or compromise Mark undeservedly by misinterpreting what you see," Millar said.

Warrick looked at him for a moment and then turned to Baker. "Good luck with the tournament today. I hope it's a success," he said.

Baker nodded, turning his golf club in his hands.

"I never depended much on luck," he said. "But that doesn't mean I'll refuse it when it comes."

"We'll take the cutoff onto Blue Diamond Road," said the deputy from behind the Cherokee's steering wheel. His name was Todd Barrett, and he was on strict one-day loan from the Clark County Sheriff's Department. "That's maybe another couple miles ahead of us."

"How long till we reach the Belcher quarry from there?" Grissom asked.

Barrett shrugged. Tanned, blond, and sinewy, he had a thin, chiseled face with sharply prominent cheekbones and wore a pair of mirrored Ray Ban aviator sunglasses.

"Depends what kind of untidiness the flood left us to deal with," he said, spurs of sunlight flashing off his shades. "Those BLM maps of yours say the camp's on that hogback west of the village, pretty much across from Spring Mountains. It's damn steep, and likely as not, whatever way your prospecting brothers used to get up there would've been washed out by water running down the slope."

"What are the odds we can find a track that's passable?"

"I'm not a betting man. But if I was, I'd say there's bound to be some dirt roads and washes that aren't blocked with debris."

Grissom was thinking Barrett at least sounded as if he knew the territory, an absolute plus considering that he was their guide for the day.

They rolled along Highway 160, Grissom in the passenger seat beside the thirtyish deputy, Sara riding in back with a pair of loaded knapsacks. Geared up with shotgun racks, a dashboard computer, and a rooftop light bar, the 4x4 patrol Jeep bringing them out into the mountains, like Barrett, was a somewhat grudgingly provided loaner from the undermanned county cops.

"At least we haven't had to deal with much road work," Sara said. She leaned forward, recalling the trip she and Gris had made to the Sunderland Trailer Court. "It looks like the water's path might have run clear of this stretch."

"I'm not sure about it being that as much as the local pols knowing who butters their bread. You have a lot of major taxpayers building their homes around here these past few years, and you should've seen how fast the state crews got down to making their repairs after the rains." Barrett glanced at her in the rearview. "Once upon a time, there was so little traffic this far out toward the valley, a boulder could have sat in the middle of the highway forever before anybody scared off the turkey vultures came to roost on it. But it's so built-up nowadays we're practically in the 'burbs . . . drive at rush hour, you might even hit an honest-to-God traffic jam."

Sara considered that. "I'm not sure whether it sounds like you prefer the boulders and turkey vultures or the taxpayers."

Barrett gave a small chuckle. "I like peace and quiet," he said. "Never had to chase down one of those buzzards for speeding or a DUI violation."

Sara smiled at that and rested back in her seat.

They rode on for a while in silence. Marked by a gas station and convenience store, the cutoff was just shy of two miles up the road, bearing out Barrett's guesstimate—yet another check mark in his favor as far as Grissom was concerned.

After turning onto Blue Diamond Road, the deputy went through an interchange outside a spread-out, busy-looking industrial park and, a little farther up, a large cactus nursery. A few

miles beyond that, the desert dramatically re-
asserted itself—erasing all signs of civilization
except strung-together utility poles, occasional
cell-phone towers, and the paved blacktop
under the Cherokee's wheels as it rolled between the furrowed western face of the hogback
to the right and, on the left, the sandstone peaks
of the mountains biting raggedly into a cloudless
azure sky.

"Okay . . . I think we might be in business,"
Barrett told Grissom after a bit. He was peering
out the right side of the windshield.

Grissom raised his eyes from the outspread
map on his thighs, gave him a mildly puzzled
glance. "We're still pretty far south of the camp,"
he said.

"But not from what looks to be a clear track we
can follow. Hang on."

The deputy abruptly swung onto the shoulder
of the road, shifted into park, and nodded toward
his glove box.

"I've got a pair of binocs in there," he said,
opening his door. "Do me a favor and hand 'em
to me—I want to show you something."

Outside the Cherokee with the CSIs a minute
later, Barrett examined the mountainside through
the glasses and then passed them to Grissom.

"Take a peek," he said. "There's a heap of mesquite about thirty yards up to the left. I'm guessing the floodwaters carried them down the ridge."

Grissom raised the double lenses to his eyes

and swung them along the trajectory of the deputy's pointing finger.

"Yeah," he said, staring at the tumbled scrub trees. "I see it."

"Now, look about another ten, fifteen feet over in that same direction, and tell me what's there."

Grissom did so and saw a shallow cut about fifteen feet wide that was apparently the product of natural erosive forces. But the parallel rows of corrugations imprinted in the dusty soil inside the cut, climbing toward the crest of the slope, were anything but natural in origin.

"Tread marks," he said. "Somebody's been up to the camp since the storm."

Barrett grunted. "Told you we'd find our track," he said.

Grissom returned the binoculars to him. "If I was a gambling man, I wouldn't bet against you," he said.

Barrett grinned. "C'mon along, folks," he said, and spun back around toward the Cherokee, with Grissom and Sara following.

Barrett managed to drive the Cherokee about a hundred feet up the slope before another tumble of uprooted mesquite trees—this pile inside the wash and larger than the deadfall he and Grissom had spotted from the road shoulder below—barred him from making any further progress.

The deputy jolted to a halt and killed the engine.

"Hope you two have your hiking legs," he said. "Because our wheels are gonna have to stay right here."

He exited the Jeep, and Grissom and Sara pushed out their doors a second afterward.

Grissom went back and leaned in to get their knapsacks, passing one of them to Sara before he strapped on his own. Barrett, meanwhile, had gone around to raise the Cherokee's hatch. From the cargo section, he took a coil of lightweight nylon rope, three trail belts, and the same number of yellow mining helmets.

"These are for you," he said, giving each of the criminalists a helmet and a belt. "You can clip the hard hats to your belts for now—no sense sweating in 'em while we're out in the hot sun."

Grissom inspected his helmet before taking Barrett's advice.

"A dual-beam headlamp?" he said.

"Got an ultraviolet light source in addition to the standard halogen bulb. In case we come across serological evidence," Barrett replied. "Mostly what prospectors do on these slopes is open-pit quarrying. But from what you told me about those crabs or whatever being in your dead man's mouth, I'm figuring your guys dug a mine goes deep into the hillside. Either that, or they found a cave that gave 'em access the underground vein system."

Grissom looked impressed. "You certainly come prepared," he said.

A large smile broke out under the deputy's angular cheekbones. "What the hell else you gonna expect from a true-blue, red-blooded western boy?" he said.

"Looks like this is our spot," Sara told Barrett. "Somebody's been busy around here."

As Grissom had gone inquisitively roaming off around an outcrop, she'd gotten her camera from her pack and crouched down to photograph a wide scattering of gravel near a roughly ten-foot-square quarry pit. It was one of a large number that had been hammered and chiseled into that part of the bare sandstone mountainside, giving it a pocked appearance reminiscent of a moonscape.

His heels crunching on the ground, Barrett came over and knelt beside her.

"The gravel would have been in tall heaps before the rain," he said. "Usually, what gem prospectors do is sieve through the raw minerals from a quarry pit right here alongside it. When the mounds build up too high, they truck them away."

Sara snapped a series of pictures with her camera, a hot bar of sunlight beating solidly on her shoulders. Though it was not yet ten o'clock in the morning, she guessed the temperature on the exposed, east-facing slope had already inched well over eighty degrees.

"The stuff's everywhere," she said with an encompassing gesture. "I'm thinking the current's force must have been tremendous."

Barrett was nodding. "Don't know if you've ever seen a river overflow its banks, but it isn't too different. These wide distribution patterns of whatever's on the surface are what happens with flash floods."

Sara considered that. "Wouldn't all the water rushing down the slope have filled the pits?"

"Hang on a sec, and I'll check something out for you." The deputy slid over the side of the pit on his heels, pushed a couple of fingers into the dirt and pebbles at the bottom, and rubbed them together. "The dirt still feels real moist—almost soggy when I stick my knuckles into it," he said, looking up at Sara. "Goes to show how saturated it was . . . which means the answer to your question's yes."

"So where did all that water go?"

Barrett shrugged. "As you can tell, it gets warm up here. Whatever doesn't soak into the ground's gonna evaporate pretty darn quick."

Sara was quiet a moment. She had briefly flirted with the notion that Adam Belcher's body could have fallen or been dumped into one of the flooded quarry pits after he was killed. But that couldn't have occurred if there were no stagnant pools. And say for argument's sake that Barrett was wrong and they'd had a chance to form . . . how would Grissom's pregger crabs have gotten down there in the pit with him? Even if the storm had washed them into the pit from wherever they lived underground, the fragile little creatures would have been too busy dying in the open sun to deposit their eggs.

One more theory nipped in the bud.

"Okay," Barrett said. He'd come scrambling up out of the pit. "From all the hammering and picking our boys were up to, I suppose we've established that they didn't take too much time out for siestas." He smacked dust and grit off the knees of his uniform trousers. "Where you want to go poking around next?"

"Inside the cave I just found."

Sara and the deputy turned at the sound of Grissom's voice to see him reappear from behind the shoulder of rock he'd rounded on his own minutes earlier.

Grissom looked at their questioning faces and poked a thumb over his shoulder. "It's maybe thirty yards back that way," he said.

Barrett nodded and reached for the mining helmet clipped to his trail belt. "I knew this would come in handy before too long," he said.

A distorted oval about two feet wide and four high, the cave mouth was recessed under a jutting stone overhang that kept it shaded from the profuse sunlight. Grissom led the others back around to it, Sara right behind him, Barrett following her by half a step.

"The interior of the cave's a tight squeeze for the first ten feet or so," Grissom said, holding an electric torch he'd taken from his backpack. "Then it widens considerably—or at least, that's how it appears from out here." He turned toward a clump of ocotillo stalks growing in the shade of the projecting ledge and motioned to Sara. "I want you to have a look at something before we go in."

She came up beside him.

"What do you see?" he said.

Sara bit her lower lip to suppress a smile and knelt. *What do you see?* It was Gris's favored line when introducing evidence or potential evidence to the investigators who trained and worked under him. Never offering what he saw but posing a guided question. Old man Socrates would have approved of his style.

All right, what?

Sprouting from crevices in the naked rock, some of the ocotillo's normally upright branches were flattened, a couple of them snapped as if they'd been stepped on, Sara observed. Shuffling closer, she produced a pair of heavy gloves from her knapsack and then moved the branching, spiny growth with one hand.

She spotted the partial shoeprints instantly—

there were three, maybe four of them, their toes pointing toward the cave entrance.

"Well, well, well," she said.

Grissom reached into his windbreaker for a photograph.

"This is a shot of Green Man's shoe bottom," he said, passing it to her.

What do you see?

Once again, she only needed to examine what Grissom had shown her for a moment.

"The outsole patterns on these partials look like matches," she said.

Sara handed him back the photo, angled her camera at the footprints, and clicked the shutter button. Meanwhile, Barrett had joined the two of them by the ocotillo patch and was leaning to inspect the shoeprint and the photograph over her shoulder.

"Those tracks are kind of dark," Barrett said. He scratched his neck. "It almost seems whoever made them walked through mud."

The material that had been on the sole of the shoe or boot had indeed struck Sara as very different from the dry, chalky sand crusting the slope. But her thoughts were on something else about the prints.

"How come there are only these few prints?" she puzzled aloud. "No others leading up to them, none leading away from them."

"I think that's a two-part question," Barrett said. He sat on his heels and gestured at the ground outside the cave opening. "There are ripples in the sand here . . . take a close look, and you'll see them."

Sara scooched over to him. They were faint but definable. "Are those watershed patterns?" she asked.

Barrett smiled. "I could tell you had some country in you," he said. "My guess is that the storm runoff came seeping into the cave at another end and then channeled out this way." He motioned downhill. "See . . . there're more ripples. The wind gets strong up here toward late afternoon, and I figure that's mostly wiped them away. But look real careful again, and you can make out how they kind of zigzag with the path the water took along the curve of the slope."

Grissom peered contemplatively downhill and then craned his head up at the rock shelf above the cave. "So you're saying the stream of floodwater from the cave opening washed out whatever prints were directly in front of it."

"Right."

"And that the overhang and ocotillo branches must have sheltered the prints *alongside* the opening from direct rainfall, and whatever other streams of water came running down the slope."

"Right again."

"All of which suggests the prints were left before the storm . . . that also right?"

Barrett nodded. "It's what seems to make sense to me."

"Me, too," Grissom said. "Which, if we're correct, leaves us with a very big unresolved question."

Sara looked at him. Her mind had been working with his—and she realized at once what he was getting at.

"If the ground up here was dry before the storm—and it would have been—how could those shoe bottoms get *wet mud* stuck to them?" she asked.

Grissom waved his electric lantern at the cave. "That's where the footsteps seem to be going," he said. "Let's follow the evidence and see if we can get some answers."

His head and back bent, Grissom edged in first. Sara was next, then Barrett.

Squeezing through the tight little cave entrance, Sara passed from bright daylight to deep, claustrophobic gloom. As she switched on her helmet lamp, she saw Grissom straighten up from his crouch. Just inside the passage, its roof must have been four feet high. A few paces in, it rose at a sharp incline.

Step, step, step, and Sara unhunkered her shoulders. Then she suddenly felt a fluttery breeze from above, glanced up, and saw the roof of the cave move.

The *roof*?

Okay, dumb, not the roof, she thought. Then what?

She squinted into an overhead darkness teeming with bats. Startled from their roosts, they swirled beneath the cave's corrugated stone ceiling in a thick cloud—dipping and tumbling through the lancing beam of her halogen light like pieces of a solid black jigsaw puzzle spilled from an overturned table.

She ducked, swatted at a few as they wheeled chaotically around her, and threw her palms in front of her face to guard it from the swooping creatures.

Pausing ahead of her in midstride, Grissom looked around at the agitated swarm. *"Corynorhinus townsendii,"* he said above their leathery flapping. None to Sara's surprise, his tone was all rapt fascination—for Grissom, this was paradise. "Townsend's big-eared bat. They use caves and mines as maternity colonies in the summer."

Great. She beat the air with her hand. "What do we do?"

"Not we," Grissom said calmly. "You and the deputy are scaring them."

Barrett took a swipe at one clinging stubbornly to his shirt. "Excuse us," he said.

"Keep still," Grissom said. "They'll settle back into their roosts."

Sara stopped moving. Barrett cursed under his breath but did likewise.

The squealing cloud of wings and fur churned around them for another minute before it finally began to subside, the bats returning to the top of the cave in bunches, folding themselves back into its recesses and crevices.

Sara waited, felt something brush against her sleeve, and flinched a little, assuming it was a straggler. But it was just Grissom.

"Come on," he whispered, nodding for her to follow him. "Don't flash your helmet lamps up at their roosts, and they'll stay put."

Moving along behind Grissom, she observed signs of miners at work, presumably before bat mating season, also presumably the Belchers. There were hammered-out gouges in the cave walls, small mounds of stone, an anodized steel bucket, a broken-tipped, casually discarded pick, egg trays for packing gems . . .

Then she heard a sound and realized she'd been hearing it since the bat attack. She glanced downward, checking out the moist crackle of her own footsteps.

"Gris—"

"I know," he said. "Take a look at this."

As he slowly passed his torch over the cave floor, Sara saw it glistening with wetness in the light. Ahead were small, scattered puddles and, running through the middle of the tunnel, a still, thin slick of water channeling toward its mouth.

She imagined Adam or Charlie stepping in the water, tracking to and from the cave with their tools, buckets, and rocks.

"Guess we know how those shoeprints got

where they are outside," Barrett said. "What I want to find now is the source of the stream."

Grissom held the lamp out in front of him and strode forward, rounding a bend in the passage. "Found it," he called back over his shoulder.

He'd kept his voice low . . . being considerate of the bats, Sara thought gladly.

She and Barrett hastened to catch up. Once they turned the bend, the cave wound farther on into the mountainside for about ten yards. At its rear was a fairly deep drip pool and, beyond it at an appreciable incline, an opening through which an almost perfect rectangle of daylight came streaming in to reflect off the pool's glassy surface.

Grissom had paused to study the opening.

"That look natural to you?" he asked Barrett.

The deputy shook his head. "Too horizontal and way too neat," he said. "It's an adit."

Grissom waited for an explanation.

"That's an opening prospectors'll dynamite into the hillside," he said. "Gives them easier access to underground mineral deposits."

Grissom stood there looking thoughtful. He dropped his pack and knelt to get an object out of a pouch—a jar with a short rubber tube on one side of its circular lid and a sort of curved metal spout or pipe on the other.

"Your turn to tell me what something is," Barrett asked, pointing to it.

Grissom rose from his haunches. "An aspirator," he said matter-of-factly, and put the loose end of the tube into his mouth.

Barrett scratched his head, watched Grissom step to the rim of the pool as if suddenly oblivious to him.

Sara came up beside the deputy, seeing his confused expression.

"He uses it for sucking up tiny animal specimens," she said.

"Huh?"

"The aspirator," she said.

Barrett looked at her for a long moment. "'Course," he said at last. "I mean, seriously, why not?"

Grissom had told the deputy it was an aspirator. But his most influential college entomology professor, a hands-on guy named Bauman, had called it a pooter, which was the traditional field collector's term Grissom preferred. Not that he would have quibbled—the simple little suction device had the same function regardless of what name you used for it.

On his knees now, he leaned over the slippery film of algae surrounding the drip pool and breathed in hard through the pooter's plastic mouth tube, drawing up dozens of tiny *Stygobromus lacicolus* amphipods he'd seen crawling around at the water's edge. A fine mesh screen element in the collection jar would prevent him from swallowing the creatures—or getting any in his lungs—and keep them trapped in the jar till he could transfer them to various other containers at the lab.

The pooter returned to his knapsack, he filled a separate vial with water from the moveless pool, capped it tightly, and took some scrapings of the algae growing around the pool's borders.

Minutes later, Grissom got to his feet, his samples gathered and carefully stored away. Hoisting his knapsack over his shoulders again, he paused for a long, thoughtful look at the adit and the shaft of invasive sunlight it allowed into the cave.

Behind him, Sara seemed to be snapping a whole lot of pictures.

He knew she'd turn something up.

Shoeprints outside the cave, more shoeprints inside.

Turning from Grissom and the drip pool, Sara had spotted them leading toward a shallow recess in the cave wall. Prints galore, and many in the tunnel weren't even partials but nice, clear, complete markings for comparison with Green Man's hiking boots . . . and not only *his* boots, she thought.

She aimed and clicked her camera, paying close attention to one thing and another about them. And then noticing something else besides.

That *something* being wheel marks, at least to her eyes. But from what?

"Looks to me like they were made by a wagon or pushcart," Barrett said, reading the interest on her face. He'd come up behind Sara as she snapped away. "Probably something the brothers used to bring rocks out of the cave."

She thought about that for almost a full minute. And took more pictures.

7

THOUGH CATHERINE WASN'T quite gaping at her computer screen when Warrick popped his head through her office door, she was close to it, the information she'd just pulled off the Internet having widened her eyes considerably.

"Cath," he said. "You're here early."

She glanced at the time readout at the bottom of her monitor. It read 10:30 A.M.

"So are you," Catherine said, thinking that neither of them was technically due in till around two in the afternoon, she being the swing-shift supervisor and Warrick being one of the CSIs assigned to her team.

Of course, if one were to be a hundred percent honest, the delineation between one shift and another got kind of noodly here at headquarters when you were working a case, which was just about always. Most often, in fact, you spent so much time gathering and analyzing crime-scene evidence that the shifts bled together so you wondered why anybody had bothered setting them up in the first place.

But Catherine guessed it was better to impose a theoretical structure to the day than none at all. If the homicidal maniacs of the world would only cooperate in practice by doing their dirty deeds in neat, punctual shifts, and clues could be discovered according to precisely defined timetables—killers and their hunters alike running their schedules in synchronous harmony—life would be marvelously divine.

". . . Mark Baker at the golf course about an hour ago," Warrick was saying.

"What about him?" Catherine frowned. "Sorry . . . my mind's in about ten different places at once."

Warrick gave her a puzzled look and then repeated himself, reminding her about the meeting he'd set up with the ballplayer and his lawyer at the charity invitational and summarizing how it had gone.

Catherine listened attentively this time. "You think he'll come in for a physical on his own volition?" she asked.

Warrick wobbled his hand in the air. "I'd put the chances at about fifty-fifty," he said. "Millar won't budge when it comes to advising him against it."

"Conscientious defense attorney that he is," Catherine said without optimism. She produced a sigh. "It'll be easier for everybody if Baker does this voluntarily. We should give him a day or so to decide before applying for a subpoena."

Warrick nodded his agreement. "So," he said, pulling a chair up to her desk. "What's with you being cooped up in here while the early birds are plucking worms out of the ground?"

"You could argue I've been doing the same thing," Catherine said. "I ran a few cross-database searches on our art connoisseur and plastic surgeon *par excellence* Dr. Layton Samuels . . . and also on his devoted wife, Eleanor."

Warrick raised an eyebrow. "Is it just my imagination that the word *devoted* sounded kind of loaded coming out of your mouth?" he asked.

Catherine sighed wearily. "According to federal records, the Samuelses are officially residents of New Canaan, Connecticut. That's where Layton practiced medicine until about ten years ago and where they still own a home," she said. "Connecticut's also the state where Eleanor Samuels made a court filing for a legal separation from her husband around the middle of last month. The grounds were spousal neglect."

Warrick made a confused face. "Hang on," he said. "Weren't the two of them at Seven Hills when you drove out there yesterday?"

"And acting like the picture of conjugal bliss," Catherine said. "Eleanor answered the front door and showed me to her husband's office. She even mentioned how involved she was with running the family business, and Layton confirmed it. He told me she handles all his appointments and computer records."

Warrick looked at her. "They wouldn't be the first couple to carry on a professional relationship after their marriage broke up," he said. "Look at The White Stripes. They made a go of it even after their divorce."

"Did they?"

Catherine smiled a little. "Have to admit," she said, "I'm not really a White Stripes fan."

"Then forget about them and think Sonny and Cher."

"If memory serves, their postdivorce show kind of tanked," she said. "But I get what you mean."

Warrick grinned. "The Samuelses have a lovey-dovey image to maintain and a lot riding on it," he said. "I don't know how many readers are gonna take *Redoing Your Spouse* seriously when they know the author split with his wife. And you have to figure they've got other book contracts in the works, lecture tours . . ."

"A mini-empire, I know," Catherine said. "Like I said, it makes sense that they'd want to keep quiet about their problems. It's just a little surprising they could actually manage it."

"Being personalities, you mean?"

"Yeah. And very visible ones."

"There are even bigger stars who find ways to keep their private lives private," Warrick said. "If it's true Samuels was stepping out with Rose Demille—or anybody else—give him credit for keeping it under wraps. There've been no public rows between him and the missus."

"And no sightings of him out on the town with other women."

"Eleanor filing papers on the East Coast probably helped, too."

"That and the fact that a legal sep doesn't stick out like a divorce motion."

"Yeah," Warrick said. "It might have slipped past the gossip trolls who go around digging their grubby hands through court records and hospital admissions."

"Might've," she repeated. "Though once *I* knew that their relationship was dissolved, or is in the process of coming apart, I started to wonder where Eleanor's been staying."

"Since she can't be living at their home."

"No, she can't," Catherine said. "Not without violating the conditions of a legal separation."

Warrick rubbed the back of his neck. "Suppose she's too careful to have bought a home in her name, huh?"

"But," Catherine said.

"But?"

"But on a hunch, I logged onto Book Highway."

"That dot-com bookseller?"

"Right," she said. "They have that peek-at-the-pages feature, where you type in a search term and it lets you read a sample of what's inside a book."

"And you found something to help tell you where Eleanor lives?"

Catherine smiled. "I looked at the copyright pages of Samuels's books. There are three of them, two registered in his own name: *Look Better, Love Better* and *Body Shaping*. But the newest book, *Redoing Your Spouse,* was copyrighted under a corporate name . . . Olga Inc."

"Olga?"

"I took a course focusing on Picasso in college," Catherine said. "It's probably no coincidence that Olga Khokhlova was the name of his first wife. What's relevant is that there's a condominium owned by Olga Inc. in Vista Tower. It was sold six months ago, when the units first went on the market."

"That's one of those four new high-rises right on Paradise Road."

Catherine nodded. "Near the Hilton, right."

"You think Eleanor's made that her residence?"

"What do *you* think?"

"I think Book Highway might've led us to Paradise when it comes to getting to the bottom of the Samuels' living arrangement."

Catherine grinned. "There's something else my potluck searches turned up," she said. "I don't know what it does or doesn't mean. But it's stuck in my mind."

Warrick gave her one of those *Don't keep me in suspense* looks.

"Layton is Eleanor's second husband," Catherine said. "Her first was Dr. Carl Melvoy, but that marriage ended back in the nineteen-nineties. November 'ninety-four, to be exact."

Warrick was still looking at her with perked interest. "Divorce?" he said.

"Death," Catherine said. "According to his published obituary in the *New York Times,* Carl passed away from sudden heart failure. The obit also mentioned that he was a noted plastic surgeon with the Upper East Side Manhattan practice of Samuels and Melvoy."

"Samuels . . . as in our *Layton* Samuels?"

Catherine nodded.

Warrick scratched his head. "You know how long Melvoy was in the ground before his widow and Samuels came together under the wedding canopy as husband and wife?"

"They were married in July of the following year."

Warrick did a quick finger count. "Eight months later," he said.

Catherine was quiet a moment. His tone of voice told her what he was trying to suggest. "There's nothing odd or suspicious about someone marrying a late spouse's friend," she finally said.

"A consoling hand turns into a loving caress?"

"Something like that," Catherine said. "Happens between people all the time. It's probably a more natural way for a bond to evolve than searching for new relationships at singles meets."

"Why not change it all tomorrow, free our love from sorrow?"

"Open up your heart to me," Catherine said.

Warrick smiled thinly. "You know the words."

"Lindsey and her friends are heavy into Nina Tyford," she said. "They've got a whole dance number worked out."

A few seconds passed as they sat smiling at each other in silence.

Catherine managed to pry her eyes from his smile. The way she'd torn herself from his arms when they'd had that awkward moment in a storm culvert investigating a case together a while back. Moments like that could be trouble. And now, as then, she pushed it into an airtight inner compartment and shut the door on it.

Shut the door with a hard *slam*.

"Okay," she said. "Let's do the checklist bit. See what we know, don't know, and maybe ought to find out next. Layton and Eleanor Samuels were both at the Cosmetic Surgery Center and Anti-aging Spa when I got there, acting . . . how did you put it? . . . . All hunky-dory?"

"Lovey-dovey," Warrick said.

"Uh-huh."

"Were the words I think I used."

"I stand corrected." Catherine gave him a look. "Anyway, there they were, the picture of togetherness. When I spoke to Layton in his office, he reinforced that impression."

"And threw cold water on any suggestion he was having an affair with Nevada Rose Demille. Though you told me Samuels did admit she'd visited his office for a consultation."

"Check," Catherine said.

"Maybe a couple of times."

"That's what he said."

"But he didn't make much of it."

"Because she never had the work done."

"Cosmetic work."

"*Whatever* sort of work it was she was interested in. Samuels wasn't specific," Catherine said.

"Didn't Samuels also tell you he and Rose might've been invited to some of the same parties for the crème de la crème of Vegas society?" Warrick asked.

"Check again."

"And then tell you they never talked."

Catherine shook her head."Not exactly," she said. "He *did* concede they might have had some chitchat."

"Chitchat?"

"That's right."

"His word or yours?"

"His," Catherine said. "Is that somehow important?"

"Could be," he said. "More than the lovey-dovey-hunky-dory controversy, anyway."

Catherine waited.

"The doc could be telling the truth," Warrick said. "But if I was a cynical investigator type, it might occur to me that he wants to make sure he's got his bases covered as far as any sightings of him with Rose Demille."

"Sightings that might look compromising."

"Like romantic trysts," Warrick said.

"Assignations."

"Intimate contacts of the kind Nova Stiles, one of Rose's oldest friends in town, implied they must have had, being that she told me they were hotsie-totsie lovers and that Samuels might even have tapped some dings out of her."

Catherine looked at him wryly. "I won't ask you about 'hotsie-totsie,'" she said.

"Thanks."

They looked at each other for another extended moment.

"Samuels and his wife are in line for a follow-up visit," Catherine said.

"You want to do it yourself, or we gonna double-team them this time?"

"I think we both should talk to them."

Warrick nodded. "Like Friday and Gannon," he said.

"Or Linc Hayes and Julie Barnes," she said.

"Coffee and cream."

"Salt and pepper."

"How about just good cop, bad cop?"

Catherine chuckled aloud. "I think we ought to make it good criminalist, bad criminalist, and quit while we're still ahead."

Warrick looked at her, smiled, and put out his hand. "Deal," he said.

"Deal," she said.

As they shook, their grip lingering for the briefest of instants, it happened again with Catherine's hardened inner vault.

Slam. Door shut. What she wanted kept out stayed out.

Catherine refused to contemplate for an instant how that entry managed to keep reopening, over and over and over, in spite of all her determination to keep it locked up tight.

Sara had just about finished her slide-show preparations when Grissom entered the forensic photography lab's square little projection room.

She gave Grissom a small nod of acknowledgment as he came through the door, finished slotting a Type II PCMCIA data-storage card into the rear of the projector, and went to the lower the room's lights. It had taken her a while to hunt down the projector, finally locating it on a table in David Hodges's lab, where it had sat after he'd apparently swiped it for some reason.

"Just in time," she said, turning the dimmer three-quarters of the way down. "I'm ready to start the show."

Grissom sat down facing the wall screen, waited.

Sara picked up her remote control and pressed a button. First up on the screen was a side-by-side comparison of the residue shoeprints she'd photographed in the ocotillo patch near the cave mouth and the outsoles of Green Man's boots—the latter a photo Grissom obviously had taken himself, since he'd been the one to bring a snapshot of the shoe bottoms to the Belcher camp with them.

Nothing wrong with giving the audience a bit of recap, she thought. Although it also might be considered a setup for the dramatic climax.

"Okay," Sara said. Her presentation moved from one photo in the series to another. "As we can see even from the partials here, the bottom markings of the boots are identical and recognizable."

Grissom nodded. Sara had placed a rigid L scale alongside the prints when she'd photographed them, the shorter base of the scale horizontal to them, the long side parallel.

"Both the work shoe and the print measure eleven and a half inches from heel to toe and are what footwear companies consider to be a wide width," Sara said. "The invoice I got from the Pakistani manufacturer called for one pair at exactly that size."

"Eleven and a half inches converts to a U.S. size twelve," Grissom said. "That right?"

"Extra-wide in this case," Sara said. "Or twelve double-E."

"Mapadi, premium leather," Grissom said.

A smile touched Sara's lips. "The prints were made by Adam Belcher," she said.

"Or Bigfoot," Grissom said.

Sara's grin widened slightly. "I've never heard a single report of Sasquatch wearing work boots," she said. "Anyway, if you look carefully at the prints—and I want to zoom in a little here so this is nice and clear—you can see that the individual characteristics of the soles also match. Notice the wear patterns?"

"On the lower right of the shoe heel," he said. "And then the instep . . ."

"Anyway, one of the other pairs Belcher ordered also measured size twelve. They were a standard D width, though."

"Charlie's boots," Grissom said.

"And by process of elimination, a third pair of boots . . ."

"A woman's model . . ."

"Was bought for Gloria Baker," Sara said. "The invoice lists them as American size six, standard width."

She thumbed the remote, and the last of her sequence of photos from outside the cave faded to black.

"Next up here are snapshots I took of the shoeprints *inside* the cave near the drip pool," she said, continuing her slide show. Again, she had placed the L scales alongside them. "The boot measures just over nine inches heel to toe. That converts to our women's size six. Regular width."

"Gloria Belcher's been in the cave," Grissom said.

Sara nodded."I did some scale compositing to create a single, spatially accurate image from several of the women's shoeprints," she said. "I wanted to verify something I'd observed in the cave. The light in there being what it was, or wasn't, it was critical to make sure my eyes weren't playing tricks on me." Another push of a button to bring her comp onto the screen. "You see anything notable about them?"

Grissom sat with his eyes narrowed, taking a close look. "The left footprint is consistently lighter than the right . . . ''

"Suggesting that the person who left the print was either hobbled or favoring that foot," Sara said.

Grissom cranked his head around to look at her. "Gloria had a limp that day at the trailer court," he said. "Did you notice?"

"I did." Sara used the remote. "There's something else," she said. "The prints go in two directions. First leading toward that recess in the wall, and then away from them."

"The same as those cart wheel tracks you photographed—and more or less behind them," Grissom said. He played with the stems of his glasses, visualizing the scene. "A few of the shoeprints are at angles to the wheels . . . *different* angles."

"As if Gloria was struggling to maneuver the cart," Sara said. "Stepping this way and that to turn it around or moving to the side . . ."

"The way you might if there was something heavy inside it." Grissom turned to look at Sara again, wondering aloud. "Like, say, a body?"

She met his gaze with her own, sharing the thought in silence.

"We'll need search warrants for Adam and Charlie Belcher's trailers," Grissom said.

"I already filled out the paperwork," Sara said. "It just needs your signature before I push it up to Jim Brass."

Grissom gave her an approving look and rose from his chair.

"I'm heading back to my office," he said. "You aren't the only one who's been busy. When you bring me those papers, I want to give you a peek at what I discovered about the algae specimens from the pool."

Sara ended her presentation with a touch of a button. Then the two CSIs stepped from the room, leaving the lights turned down in their haste.

When he searched the photo lab for the projector an hour later, Hodges would trip over its electrical cord in the dimness. And while he barely avoided knocking over the projector, the tech would painfully bruise his left toe stumbling against the bolted-down legs of a table.

Not having the slightest clue which of the criminalists at the lab might be to blame, he would make sure to cover his all bases by loudly and vehemently cursing every last, stinking one of them.

"Have you ever met my friend John Tuttle?" Grissom asked Sara. "He's a professor of botany and the phycologist with the Nevada Division of Environmental Protection?"

About five minutes after they left the projection room, she stood with Grissom over one of his binocular microscopes.

"Tell you the truth," she said with a shake of her head, "I didn't know the agency had a resident algae specialist."

Grissom carefully positioned a specimen slide under the microscope's revolving nose turret. "They didn't always," he said. "But two or three years ago, Lake Mead was overrun with a type of invasive plant known as *Myriophyllum spicatum.* It's also known as Eurasian water milfoil, or just plain milfoil. It has a kind of wispy, feathery appearance and tolerates a wide range of freshwater environments. Hot climates, cold climates, it's just plain tough to kill. Pet stores used to sell it because it's so hardy. That makes it popular with hobbyists, who put it in their aquarium tanks because fish like to graze on it."

Sara grunted and watched Grissom carefully secure his slide in place with stage clips.

"About half a decade before Lake Mead's infestation, the same problem with milfoil occurred in Lake Tahoe," he said, and turned on the illuminator. "In fact, it's happened in lakes and rivers ranging from Canada down to Florida. The plant may have been originally introduced by people dumping and flushing water from their fish tanks into local drainage systems. Or it might have clung to the keels and motors of pleasure boats and entered our water bodies that way. However it happened, it spelled trouble. Milfoil proliferates rapidly, forming into dense mats that choke off the growth of other plants and upset entire native habitats. It also interferes with the water intake of hydroelectric generators. I could go on for hours explaining the environmental and economic costs of an infestation."

Sara looked at him. "And I'm sure you would—except for my reminding you that we have work to do, starting with your signing off on the search-warrant application," she said. "Not to be a spoilsport, but I'm also waiting for you to explain how all this ties in with Adam Belcher."

Grissom peered briefly through the microscope's eyepieces and cranked the lens down to begin focusing.

"When the Tahoe situation arose, Tuttle was enlisted to help determine the effects of milfoil on the lake's ecosystem," he said. "After he conducted his initial tests, he was surprised to discover that the plant was actually releasing allelopathic chemicals into the water."

Sara raised her eyebrows. "They're deadly to other kinds of algae?"

"Right," Grissom said. "The toxic polyphenols are specifically gallic acid, pyrogallic acid, ellagic acid, and catechin, and it's your blue and blue-green algae and diatoms that are most susceptible to them." He tinkered some more with his microscope's focus knobs. "John fought off a government committee's plan to use herbicides to kill off the milfoil, arguing that it would open up an environmental Pandora's box by eliminating indigenous plants and animals. Eventually, as the lesser of several evils, he introduced a species of beetle and also a crayfish that feed on the milfoil, knowing that would bring about their own ecological imbalances since they were also foreign life-forms. But—"

Sara tapped Grissom's arm to interrupt him.

"Yes?" he said, glancing up from the scope to look at her.

"The Belcher connection," she said. "Please, please, pretty please."

Grissom cleared his throat. With his baby face, he looked a bit like a child who realized he'd broken a rule without having the slightest idea why it had been imposed on him. "In the process of carrying out his investigation, John took what wound up being a comprehensive inventory of the algae that naturally occur in Nevada's water bodies," he said. "The most prevalent species statewide was *Pyramichlamys*. It's the type that overwhelmingly showed up in our water samples from Fairmark Lake."

Sara looked at him, remembering. "Greg collected them the day Belcher was found by those cleanup workers," she said.

Grissom moved away from the microscope, gesturing for Sara to take his place behind it.

She lowered her head to study the slide he had mounted on the stage.

"Is the algae on this slide from one of Greg's samples?" she asked.

"No," Grissom said. "You're looking at a culture of *Stichococcus bacillaris*. An entirely different species of algae from the scrapings you removed from Belcher's hands and face."

She grunted. "Would it usually be found in the lake?"

"Almost never," he said. "It's a form of cave algae, rare throughout Nevada, and I collected it from the stone around the drip pool." He paused. "According to John, it's among the few that can thrive in very minimal light levels . . . say, the amount that might enter through an adit."

Sara raised her eyes from the microscope and saw Grissom holding out another slide.

"Here," he said. "Have a look."

She placed the second specimen slide under the microscope's objective lenses . . . and instantly realized the culture she was studying was indistinguishable from the sample on the slide she'd just *removed*.

Sara turned toward Grissom, a look of comprehension dawning across her features.

"Belcher's body didn't pick up its coating of algae in Fairmark Lake," she said. "This pretty well goes to show it grew and spread on him in the drip pool."

"Pretty well," Grissom agreed.

"But how do you think he got from one place to the other? Do you really believe it's possible the floodwaters could have washed him all the way down into the lake?"

"Possible . . . yes," Grissom said. "As for the question of *how* possible it might be, that's one I don't have enough information to answer."

"You have an idea where to get hold of it?"

He gave her one of his enigmatic smiles. "Maybe we can start a few doors down the hall," he said.

"Warrick!"

He had barely left Catherine's office when he heard Grissom call his name, and he turned to see Gris hustling in his direction.

He waited in the corridor a few steps outside Cath's door.

"You're here early," Grissom said, catching up.

Warrick looked at him. He was thinking that Gris, being the night-shift supervisor, was out and about even earlier than Catherine and himself, relatively speaking.

"Déjà vu," he muttered, scratching his ear.

"Paramnesia," Grissom said.

"What?" Warrick said.

"I heard you say 'déjà vu,'" Grissom said.

Warrick kept looking at him. "Right," he said.

"People tend to give a preternatural or mystical significance to the phenomenon," Grissom said. "But the nineteenth-century psychiatrist Emil Kraepelin used the term *paramnesia* essentially to explain it as a brain hiccup."

"Oh."

Grissom rubbed his chin thoughtfully. "Kraepelin never received the same historical prominence as Freud. In fact, they were dismissive of each other. Probably because Kraepelin took a hard scientific view of psychiatric disorders and aberrations . . . saw virtually all of them as pathologies with biological causes, as opposed to Freud's philosophical constructions, which tended to strike a more popular chord. Scientists hadn't developed the medical tools at the time to examine and map brain functions adequately—"

"Boss . . ."

Grissom looked at him and cleared his throat. "I simply tend to prefer the term—"

"*Paramnesia*," Warrick finished.

"Correct."

Warrick didn't say anything. *Potato, potahto, tomato, tomahto, let's call the whole thing off*, he thought, certain the brothers Gershwin must have been having a morning a whole lot like his when they'd written their song.

"So," he said finally, "Kraepelin's theories aside . . ."

"I need you to help me out with something," Grissom said.

Warrick looked at him. "Now? Catherine and I were about to look into some things about Nevada Rose—"

"You mean the case involving the dead woman," Grissom said.

"Uh-huh."

"As opposed to *the* Nevada Rose," Grissom said. "Which is the gemstone connected to the Green Man investigation."

Warrick felt a sudden throb in both temples. "Right," he said, thinking he'd definitely have to find an aspirin or three to chew on once they were through with their conversation. "So, which do you want me to give you an assist with?"

Grissom, for his part, was forging right ahead. "The Green Man–slash–Nevada Rose case," he said. "It shouldn't take long. Greg has already compiled the necessary geographic charts and tables, including satellite images of the terrain, photo reference of the cave's interior dimensions and features, and other variables."

"What terrain are you talking about," Warrick asked. "What *cave*?"

Grissom's eyes narrowed. "Have you been listening to me at all?" he said.

Warrick took a breath. "Yeah," he said.

"Because you seem inattentive."

"Well, I'm not sure I'd call it that." Forget crunching on aspirin, Warrick was about ready for something significantly stronger. "It's just that you could say I'm up to my ears in another case here. With Catherine. And I was about to make a phone call to arrange for us to—"

"Come on."

Grissom clamped a hand on his elbow and practically spun him around in a full circle.

"Hey!" Warrick flinched. "Where you taking me?"

"Over to Greg, where else?" Grissom said, dragging him along the hall. "The sooner the two of you get to work on this, the faster Catherine can have you back."

"Dum–dum–dum–deedee–deedee–dee . . ." Greg Sanders hummed, seated in front of a computer monitor the approximate size of the Australian continent.

As Warrick took the chair next to him, spinning it around to sit with his legs straddling the backrest, he recognized the tune coming out of his mouth as the Kermit the Frog ode to being green that had seemingly sunk its hooks into the soft brain tissues of everyone at the criminalistics lab.

Warrick waited a second for Sanders to acknowledge his presence. When, not the smallest bit to his surprise, it didn't happen, he frowned and tapped him on the shoulder.

"Are you gonna let me know exactly what we're doing in front of this computer, or am I supposed to read your mind?" he said.

Greg's fingers kept flying over his keyboard. "I thought the boss already explained it to you," he said.

"Well, he didn't," Warrick said. "Except for mentioning some charts—"

"Bureau of Land Management charts of the Spring Mountains, Red Rock Canyon, and Humboldt-Toiyabe National Forest, right." Greg paused in his tapping. "You want the problem in a nutshell?"

"Think that's what I was asking."

Greg sighed. "We start with an unidentified dead body floating with the swans in Fairmark Lake," he said.

"Green Man," Warrick said.

"Whom we are later *able* to identify to a fair degree of certainty as a gem hunter named Adam Belcher," Greg said. "Though I actually prefer the name Green Man, for what that's worth."

Warrick looked at him with pointed impatience. "I don't have all day, man."

"Okay, okay," Greg said. "Cutting right ahead to this morning, we follow dedicated and heroic criminalists Gil Grissom and Sara Sidle, along with some local-yokel deputy . . . into a cave up in the mountains near Blue Diamond, at a site where Adam 'Green Man' Belcher and his brother staked a prospecting claim."

"They find any evidence Belcher was killed there?"

Greg shrugged. "You'd have to ask them," he said. "What they did find was evidence—strong evidence—that Belcher was dumped in a drip pool inside the cave."

"And what would that be?"

"Hmm?"

"The evidence."

"I thought you didn't have time to hear the full story from me."

"I don't," Warrick said. "If I don't have to."

"In my humble view, it isn't necessary," Greg said. "But if you do want it, I'd refer you to the Sidle slide show, which I believe is even now being screened down the hall in the photo analysis lab."

"Look, I'm just trying to figure out what I'm doing here."

"And I was just getting around to it," Greg said somewhat curtly. He blew air through his mouth. "Some of the evidence—a portion only of significance to you and me in terms of setting up our specifically assigned problem—is that the pool was brimming over with a species of amphipod that only thrives in our local Nevada caves."

"Uh-huh."

"A rare type belonging to the *same* ugly little

white species that deposited a slimy glopping cluster of eggs in Belcher's mouth."

"Uh-huh."

"A type that's incapable of surviving—and that certainly wouldn't be stimulated into egg-laying behavior—outside a sunless underground environment."

Warrick looked at him. "So you're saying that Grissom and Sara think the dead man's body became a host for the eggs in the drip pool and then somehow got transported down the mountainside—"

"Washed."

"Huh?"

"Got *washed* down the mountainside," Greg said.

"Okay, right, *washed* down the mountainside into the man-made lake."

Greg nodded. "Based on that and other evidence we don't need to worry about right now, what they postulate is that Green Man's—that is, Belcher's—watery voyage occurred during the flood a couple of weeks back," he said. "The thing we *do* have to concern ourselves with is determining whether that hypothesis can be proven out. And short of re-creating the flood, a tall order unless you happen to be really good at doing a rain dance, the only option we have is to generate a computer sim."

Warrick thoughtfully scratched his stubbled chin. "So that's what Grissom's charts and sat relief maps are about."

"There you go," Greg said. "Our task at hand."

Warrick sat there considering that a moment.

"What kind of software you using?" he said, and tipped his head toward the computer monitor.

Greg gave him a half-smile. "Thought you would never ask," he said. "A couple days ago, Nick and I were working with Profiler."

"The chromatography–facial ID software."

"Right," Greg said. "That's what we used to help get a positive make on Belcher in the first place. And it got me wondering about the possibility of another type of fusion software. Something that might combine the CG applications movie studios use for realistic special effects like tidal waves, whirlpools, and plain old stormy seas with the kind of software developers use to figure out drainage for construction projects nowadays."

Warrick looked at him. "Don't even try to sell me on the idea that you developed a program in—what—like two or three days?"

"Have to be honest," Greg said. "I knew a friend of mine at MIT was already screwing around with a prototypical version. Just wasn't sure how far along he'd gotten with it. So I gave him a call and asked."

"And?"

Greg patted the top of his computer. "I've got the program installed in here," he said. "We're locked and loaded."

Warrick was quiet a few seconds. "The movement of liquid's a seriously complex process," he said. "It's gonna be impacted by all kinds of forces. There's gravity, for one thing."

"And friction, for another," Greg said, thinking along with him.

"Plus landscape features, fluctuations in the speed and direction of the wind . . ."

"The amount and force of the rain that was hitting it as it surged . . ."

"Any kind of natural and artificial boundaries or barriers it might have come up against . . ."

"Or overflowed . . ."

"Like dams and storm conduits, to name a couple, not to mention everything from homes to the cars in front of them . . ."

"Even the composition, texture, aridity, and porosity of the soil and other material it might have passed over . . ."

"Or *picked up* while it was rushing downhill," Warrick said. "And say we manage to plot the course of the water. Tough enough, right? Next, we'd have to factor in how the dead man's body would interact with it—and with other aspects of the path it traveled."

"Definitely poses another set of hydrodynamic problems," Greg replied.

"A whole 'nother set," Warrick said. "Every valley shall be filled, and every mountain and hill shall be brought low, and the crooked shall be made straight, and the rough ways shall be made smooth."

"Something tells me that ain't the great musical poetess Nina Tyford," Greg said.

"Nope."

"Or even Jerry Garcia."

Warrick smiled thinly and turned toward the computer screen. "C'mon on, boy genius," he said. "We better get our science-fair project cooking."

8

"HERE SHE COMES," Catherine said.

"So far, so good," Warrick said.

"It better be—we've been here forever," Catherine said.

Warrick glanced at his wristwatch, thinking it was maybe closer to an hour, but he caught her drift. It had damn near *felt* like an eternity since they had planted themselves near the Vegas Hilton's main entrance across Paradise Road from the seven-hundred-foot aerial thrust of Vista Tower. Though standing there among the pushing, shoving concentration of tourists outside the hotel had put them at a fairly direct and inconspicuous vantage for observing the condo development's vehicle gate, it was no fun at all.

His eyes attentive behind a pair of sunglasses, Warrick watched the silver Mercedes-Benz roadster pass them on its way to the gate. The rear vanity plate read "Bodyspa." Behind the steering wheel was Eleanor Samuels.

The Benz turned up the drive and paused at the security gate as it swung inward on an electronic command. After a moment, Eleanor drove through onto a paved drive and stopped again. A valet appeared from the high-rise, went around to her door, and opened it to help her out.

Wearing a black mid-length skirt and matching heels, she took some shopping bags from the back of the car and carried them into the building.

"I'm surprised she didn't have the valet bring 'em up to her once he parks the Benz," Warrick said.

Catherine smiled. "Those bags are from Saks Fifth Avenue," she said.

"So?"

"So it's hard to separate a girl from her goodies," Catherine said. "If they were groceries, he'd be loaded down like a pack mule."

Warrick made a face. "Stupid me," he said. "Goes to show why I'm divorced."

Catherine smiled again and was quiet for a second or two. "We should give Eleanor a chance to settle in," she said. "Kick off her shoes, fix a martini, turn on the stereo, and sink into the couch."

Warrick nodded, and they waited some more among the fizzy, kinetic swarm of tourists.

After about ten minutes, they crossed Paradise and turned in the opposite direction from the tower's vehicle gate, heading toward the walk-in entrance. A front path led up to it between parallel lanes of palm trees, and an alert uniformed doorman stood inside a wide, bright, glossy-floored vestibule.

He watched the CSIs cautiously as they approached. "Can I help you?"

Catherine displayed her identification to the guy at the door. As he looked it over, Warrick glanced up to see a bank of remotely operated video cameras. Besides the doorman, he knew there would be a guard—or guards—keeping watch on the entry from a security station elsewhere in the building.

"How do I know this isn't a counterfeit?" the doorman said, still examining Catherine's badge.

She shrugged. "You can take our word for it," she said. "Or make a call to check us out if you feel like wasting time."

"*Or* ask one of your security boys."

"What?"

Warrick motioned toward the video cams. "They've gotta be moonlighting LVPD," he said. "Ask them, they'll give you reason to believe."

The doorman expelled a breath and raised his eyes from the badge.

"Okay," he said. "What can I do for you?"

"We need Eleanor Samuels's apartment number, and we need for you to let us into the building," Catherine said. "Then we need for you to make sure that you don't buzz up to let her know we're here."

He studied her face for a long moment and finally aquiesced. "Unit Thirty-seven C," he said, pushing open the inner door. "Take the first escalator to your right."

Catherine nodded and went through, Warrick following a step behind.

"Yo," the doorman said, still holding open the door.

Warrick paused.

"This is none of my business, okay?" the doorman said. "You didn't even see me here when you came in."

Warrick removed his glasses, pretended to scan the vestibule, and nodded. "Can't see a thing when I take these off," he said, and turned into the lobby.

As Catherine and Warrick would have thought, Unit 37C was on the thirty-seventh of Vista Tower's forty-four sky-kissing floors. The nameplate insert under the doorbell button didn't say anything about Olga Inc. Nor, Catherine noted, did it mention Jacqueline, Geneviève, Françoise, Marie-Therese, or any of Picasso's other known lovers.

It also didn't list Eleanor Samuels as the apartment's occupant.

The nameplate was plainly and simply blank.

Catherine rang once, then stood outside the door and listened, heard movement behind it, and waited for Eleanor to answer the bell.

Nothing.

Catherine rang a second time.

Waited again.

And heard some more quiet shuffling behind the door.

Still no answer from Eleanor, though.

This hardly came as a shock to the CSIs. Every indication was that Mrs. Samuels had wanted to keep her hideaway—or possibly it was her new permanent address—as private as could be. But they had not come here to stand out in the hallway because she wanted to keep secrets. They were investigating a woman's death, and were in no mood for games or evasions.

Catherine knocked on the door, rapping it hard with her knuckles.

"Mrs. Samuels, we know you're home," she said. "This is Catherine Willows from the LVPD. I visited your husband at Seven Hills the other day."

She waited a third time and finally heard the clattering of the lock. Then the door opened inward about a third of the way, Eleanor Samuels appearing there in the space between the apartment and the outer hall.

"What are you doing here?" she said, standing barefoot behind the partially open door, having changed from the skirt she'd worn outside into a pair of loose-fitting Adidas sweatpants.

No martini glass in her hand, Catherine thought. But she'd probably have left that inside in the living room if she'd prepared one. And if not, Catherine figured she'd still been close enough with her prediction to feel satisfied with herself.

"Mrs. Samuels, we need to talk," she said.

Eleanor shook her head. "I'm sorry," she said, glancing over Catherine's shoulder at Warrick, then back at Catherine, her face full of surprise and confusion. "I don't . . . I don't know how you found me. But this is a corporate apartment. My husband and I keep it for our more prominent patients. People who want to recuperate from surgery without drawing attention to themselves, you know. I—I just stopped in for a while to check on things and am on my way out."

Catherine nodded her chin down at the floor. "In your bare feet?"

Eleanor looked at her. "You caught me while I was about to start getting dressed," she said. "I must have fallen asleep . . ."

Catherine locked eyes with her, dropped her voice several notches in volume. "We saw you come in about fifteen minutes ago," she said. "Carrying an armload of shopping bags from Saks."

Eleanor looked at her for another long moment but said nothing.

"We prefer not to embarrass you, Mrs. Samuels," Catherine said. "We very honestly would like to avoid that if possible. But we will if you leave us no other option."

Eleanor's face had suddenly turned pale. "What's this about?" she said, an audible tremor in her voice now. "I need to know what . . ."

"Mrs. Samuels, we won't stand out here all day," Catherine said. "What is it you intend to do?"

There was a long silence, Eleanor Samuels staying put in the door to the apartment, the CSIs standing in the hallway outside, none of them showing a willingness to budge an inch.

Looking at the determined expression on Catherine's face, Eleanor finally relented.

"Okay," she said, pulling open the door. "You'd better come inside."

Eleanor Samuels apparently shared her husband's affinity for fine art, and enormously *expensive* fine art, at that.

Entering the living room, Catherine was struck by a huge Georgia O'Keeffe canvas on the wall, a yellow cactus flower blooming skyward against the dun-colored desert sand.

She remained in front of the painting a moment as Warrick stepped past her for a circumspect look around.

"Fabulous, isn't it?" Eleanor said, moving up alongside her.

"Yes," Catherine said. "I've always wanted to visit the Ghost Ranch."

Eleanor gave a quick smile, but her eyes had the same uneasy look they'd had peering out at the CSIs from her doorway.

"Have you?" she said. "I've made the trip and would recommend it. It gave me tingles to see the desert landscapes where O'Keeffe did so much of her work . . . there's something wonderful and inspirational about her ability to capture such delicate beauty amid their harshness."

Catherine nodded, then turned from the canvas and scanned the room. On her right was a large red sofa. Beyond that a hallway with a dressing room at the end, its door partially open.

She saw Warrick looking through the door and knew he'd already noticed the same things that had just caught her eye—the assortment of cosmetics on an antique vanity, the Saks shopping bags resting atop a matching armoire.

"Did you do the decorating yourself?" she said, returning her gaze to Eleanor's face.

"I had help locating what I wanted," Eleanor said. "But yes, I did, for the most part. We—Layton and I—do whatever we can to make our patients feel as comfortable as possible."

Catherine looked at her. *Here we go again.*

"Your patients?"

Eleanor nodded. Very briskly, the way she'd smiled. Her eyes still nervous and uneasy.

"As common as it's become in our society, people still aren't sure what to expect from aesthetic surgery," she said, almost as if by rote. "The purpose of our books and television appearances isn't just to inform them of its benefits but spread an awareness of what to expect before opting for any procedure." She paused. "One thing we're very up-front about is stating that some of them can be followed by a recuperative period of several days or weeks."

It occurred to Catherine that Mrs. Samuels could easily have been rehearsing those lines backstage in the green room of some morning talk show. But while it was tempting to break into her little infomercial, Catherine decided instead to give her some added rope, figuring it would probably pay off to find out what her whole cock-and-bull story was going to be.

"With so many of Layton's clients these days being popular music stars and other personalities, we've become sensitive to their exceptional needs," she rattled on. "Many of them want a postop retreat, a safe house where they can get away from the flashbulbs while they're healing . . . and we provide it right here along with visiting nurses, attendants, physical therapists, and—"

Having heard about all she could take, Catherine gave Warrick a glance signaling him to interrupt.

"Look," he said, stepping over. "We know this place isn't for your clients."

She looked at him, her eyes widening. "I don't understand why you keep suggesting that," she said. "I told you why I'm here. A patient recently vacated after a stay, and I just stopped in to make sure everything was in order."

Catherine made subtle eye contact with War-rick again. It was her turn now. Time to bring the pressure down a notch.

"Mrs. Samuels . . . Eleanor," she said. "We know you filed for a separation from your hus-band . . ."

"And you think it had something to do with Rose Demille."

"Didn't it?"

Eleanor shrugged. "Layton told me why you came to see him at the spa," she said. "That you questioned him about possibly having a relation-ship with her. I'm guessing it's why you're here right now. To ask if I know anything about it."

So at the very least, Eleanor knew her husband was suspected of being involved with another woman, Catherine thought. But forget that—based on the separation she'd initiated, she most likely knew without a *doubt* that he'd been hav-ing an affair. And now the woman he had been cheating with was dead. And Eleanor was cover-ing for him.

Catherine wondered how best to draw her out. She was used to taking all sorts of different ap-proaches with all sorts of different people and got the sense that Eleanor Samuels might be recep-tive to a soft touch.

"It's embarrassing . . . humiliating to be be-trayed by someone you love," she said. "I can ap-preciate what you're feeling."

Eleanor stared at her. "Can you?" she said,

her tone at once angry and defensive. "Can you, really?"

Catherine nodded, maintaining eye contact. Preparing to share what she would rather not be sharing. To meet this total stranger's deceptiveness with a painful truth in order to work some sort of connection somewhere.

"Yes, I can," she said. "I've been there myself. Trust me. And I know that whatever reason you've got for covering up for your husband is only bound to hurt you in the long run."

They stood looking at each other in the middle of the room, neither of them saying anything, Eleanor's lower lip beginning to tremble the way it had when she'd come to answer the door.

"Let's start over, talk right here," Catherine said. Calm, calm. Sugar to Warrick's spice, Gannon to his Friday. Or maybe just one woman to another. *Trust me.* "We'd rather not have to do this in an interrogation room at police headquarters . . . you don't need that. But we do want a clear picture of what's going on here."

Eleanor finally motioned Catherine and Warrick toward the sofa, waiting for them to lower themselves onto its cushions before she sat down at the other end, her back pressing against the armrest.

Catherine looked at Eleanor. Waited. Giving her thoughts and emotions an opportunity to thread their way through the silence.

"It isn't what you think," Eleanor finally said.

She produced a humorless chuckle. "Well, the part about my husband and Rose Demille is . . . it would be ridiculous for me to go on denying it. I'm sure you have your sources of information. But you're wrong as far as my reason for trying to keep our separation secret."

Catherine waited some more. She could practically feel Warrick thinking along with her, recalling what they had discussed in her office back at headquarters.

"It was a business decision, wasn't it?" she said. Not tiptoeing around here, coming right out with it. "You wanted to guard your image."

"Protect it, yes." Eleanor was nodding. "We have an obligation. Not only to ourselves but to the franchise. The staffers we employ, the publishers who've invested in our books, the cosmetics companies that pay for our endorsements, and the ordinary people who've seen us on television and come to trust our advice for improving their lives."

How altruistic, Catherine thought. Not a word about keeping the millions of dollars they made from all those book deals, patients, and endorsements flowing into their corporate accounts. It was amazing Eleanor didn't sprout wings and a halo and go soaring up toward the pearly gates.

"About your husband and Rose Demille," she said, wanting to get the conversation back on point. "When did you first find out about them?"

Eleanor took a deep breath. "There's a thin

line between suspicion and knowing," she said. "If you've really had a similar experience in your life, I shouldn't have to explain. Layton went through the stages. The evasiveness. The excuses for spending time away from home. The nights he was supposed to be at meetings that didn't exist."

"And then getting careless," Catherine said.

Eleanor nodded. "Leaving a note from her in his sport coat. Storing her number on his cell phone, charging gifts to our joint credit-card account. There comes a time when the signs stack up so high it's impossible to avoid toppling them over. I've wondered if perhaps they're deliberately left out around you. So he can be relieved of the burden of having to tell you the truth. So that he can pretend he wants to make things right . . . leave it to you to say good-bye because he can't work up the nerve."

Catherine was aware of Eleanor using the disassociative *you,* a subconscious mechanism that allowed people to talk about their deepest personal wounds with a greater degree of remove. Work for the LVPD as long as she had, listen to as many stories as she had, and it was *you, you, you,* dozens of them for every *I.*

"Do I understand that you confronted your husband about his relationship with Rose Demille?" she asked.

Eleanor shook her head. "Eventually," she said. "At first, I kept things to myself. I knew their togetherness would have been fleeting."

"How could you have been so sure?"

Eleanor shrugged. "That woman, she was the type who would always be looking to upgrade," she said. A bitter edge to her words now. "Rose Demille is dead, and I know I must sound cold-hearted. But it's the simple reality."

Catherine looked at her. "How did your husband take it when you stopped trying to wait out the affair and told him what you knew?"

"There was everything you would expect from him. A round or two of weak denials and then the obligatory apologies for his lies." Eleanor produced another harsh approximation of a laugh. "It's the nature of the male species, all those guilty 'I'm sorrys' and admissions of responsibility. They're just superficial twitches. Like the knee-jerk reflex. They have nothing to do with conscience or a genuine sense of right and wrong."

Catherine didn't have to look at Warrick to know exactly what he was thinking. She remembered his jaundiced reaction when she'd told him about Eleanor and Layton hooking up within months after her first husband—and his medical partner—died of a coronary. His unsubtle suggestion that Eleanor and her second spouse might have gotten warm and cozy with each other *before* Carl's demise. Finally, she could not help but recall the personal skid Warrick had taken not so very long ago, after discovering his own wife—now his ex—had been fooling around with another man. Ask his opinion of which sex was more inclined toward marital infidelity, and he would insist that cheating and deception were the nature of the *human* species, male and female, all aboard.

"Did Layton give any indication he'd break things off with Rose?" Catherine said now, snapping her full attention back to Samuels's wife.

"No," she said. "She really had him hooked. Even when she was out clubbing with that baseball player . . . the one they say was with her the night she died."

"So seeing them step out together in public didn't bother your husband?"

"You'd have to ask him," Eleanor said. "Certainly, he was able to accept it. I remember Layton practically laughing off a gossip-magazine article about Rose and the ballplayer."

"And you didn't wonder why?"

Eleanor shook her head. "If so, I didn't ask him about it," she said. "What was its bearing on my situation? Certainly, he was able to accept her other dalliances. Once during an argument, Layton even told me he'd found a 'soul mate' in her . . .'' Eleanor let her voice trail and gave one of her small, weary shrugs. "Don't you hate that term, Ms. Willows? Don't you just *despise* it?"

Catherine felt that might be putting it a touch too strongly, though she easily might have agreed that it was one of the more starry-eyed, adolescent New Age terms that had entered the popular language in recent times.

Right now, however, she wasn't inclined to offer that or any other opinion to Eleanor Samuels. Instead, she was thinking that she and Warrick had already extracted a good amount of information from her, at least for the present, and that they had better refrain from getting greedy and quit while they were ahead of the game.

She shot Warrick a communicative glance, and they rose from the sofa, Catherine thanking Mrs. Samuels for her time and cooperation before the CSIs let her show them across the living room and out of the apartment.

As they stepped back out into the hall, Eleanor hesitated for the briefest of moments before shutting her door behind them, standing there in the entry almost as she had when they'd arrived.

"Ms. Willows?" she said in a hushed voice.

Catherine paused, looked around at her.

"This charade I've been carrying on . . . it hasn't been one of my shining moments," Eleanor said. "I just want you to know I'm aware of that."

Catherine gave a slight nod but did not comment. She simply had no idea what to say to her.

And then Eleanor closed and locked the door. Over and out. Catherine stood there a moment, not moving, staring at the blank nameplate below the doorbell, before she finally took a deep breath and turned away from it, joining Warrick as he strode down the hallway to the elevators.

Not quite forty-eight hours after their first drive over to the Sunderland Trailer Court, Sara and Grissom were heading back there on the barely passable, flood-ruined roads east of downtown Vegas, feeling their vertebrae jolt increasingly and alarmingly out of whack with every chunk of potholed, washed-out, and by turns collapsed and heaved-up blacktop they had somehow to find a way to traverse.

What made this evening's return trip very different for them—besides its grievously compounding toll on their spines and Gris's shock absorbers as they rattled along—was the fact that they were now armed with search warrants for Charlie and Adam Belcher's respective mobile homes and also that they were being escorted by a couple of LVPD patrol cars just in case Gloria Belcher launched into another certifiably hysterical performance of the type she'd put on last time around.

And that wasn't all. There were some other very significant things that distinguished this trip from the previous one. On their last venture out to the trailer park, Grissom and Sara had been reasonably certain that the Fairmark Lake floater Greg Sanders had dubbed Green Man was indeed and truly the gemstone prospector Adam Belcher, owing to Profiler's facial reconstruction and the positive identification provided by Professors Gaines and Evercroft down at Aldren. Rattling along right now, they were absolutely, one hundred percent convinced of that initial ID and moreover were firmly persuaded that Adam had met his premature demise at the Belcher mining camp, then either fallen or gotten dumped into the drip pool at the back of the onsite cave, and *then* been washed off and away into Fairmark Lake during the near-biblical flooding of two—now going on three—weeks past.

Flipping on his headlights in the early evening twilight, Grissom mentally reviewed the evidence that bore out that rather bizarre sequence of events. There were Sara's comparisons of the shoeprints from the Belcher camp with the heel and sole markings on the dead man's premium-quality Pakistani leather work boots. There was Grissom's own absolute determination that the *Stygobromus lacicolus* arthropods he had gathered at the Belcher site's drip pool were the same species of egg-laying critter that had used the floater's mouth as a hatchery for its impending brood. And there was the perfect microscopic match between the algae Grissom had collected in the cave and the green vegetable fuzz that had rampantly overgrown on the floater's hands and face to earn him his unfortunate *Sesame Street*–inspired sobriquet.

Last but not least, adding to that evidentiary picture, there was the computerized water-flow animation Warrick and Sanders had worked up to demonstrate in visually dramatic fashion—and to a high degree of arithmetical probability—the likeliest path Belcher's dead body would have taken as it was swept downslope from the over-flowing drip pool into the artificial lake far below.

Grissom spotted the access road to the trailer court up ahead and motioned out his window to signal the uniforms behind him that they were approaching the turnoff. Then he pulled his arm back inside and thought some more. Still very much a matter of conjecture was what Gloria Belcher's shoeprints were doing in the cave and why she had been having a wrestling match with a cart or wheelbarrow of some kind near the drip pool. And, of course, the biggest unanswered questions—those at the nub and hub of the inves-tigation presently wreaking havoc on whatever was left of his car's suspension system—remained very much at the front of his curious mind: What were the circumstances of Adam Belcher's death? And who, if anyone besides Belcher himself, was responsible for it?

Grissom had expected to find everything at the trailer court in about the same bad shape it had been in the other day, and what he saw as he drove through confirmed it, the neglect and storm damage combining to make for a scene of dismal shabbiness.

But something about the Belchers' plot had changed. He noticed it the moment the battered, rusty Skyline Nomad came into sight. Gone now was the front deck made out of worn wooden planks in front of it.

He glanced across the seat at Sara. "What do you think's up with the deck?"

"I was wondering that, too," she said. "It doesn't necessarily mean anything."

But then again, maybe it did, and the looks they exchanged said they both knew it.

The deck hadn't been fixed in place. It was rigged to come apart in sections. So, Grissom thought, the Belchers might have decided to bring it inside for storage or repair. Or they might have done it with intentions of vacating the plot.

He cut his ignition and waited for the two police cruisers to pull up behind him.

"Okay." He looked at Sara again. "Ready?"

She nodded.

The CSIs opened their doors and got out, saw the unis piling from their patrol cars.

It was a few minutes after six o'clock, nearly dark out, and Grissom could see lights from inside the trailer come seeping around the sides of its drawn shutters.

Probably, then, somebody was home. But tonight Grissom had no concern about whether anyone would be. He had the search-and-seizure warrants in his pocket and could have the cops knock down the door as a contingency.

In a sense, he thought, it would make things easier if the place was deserted—possibly not better, though. He was smart enough to know that. He and Sara had to get what they needed.

Her probable antics aside, they wanted Gloria there.

"You want us to go in with you?" one of the cops said, walking up to Grissom.

He considered that.

"You guys hang back a little," he said. "I'll take first crack."

"All right."

Grissom went up toward the trailer, waving for Sara to stay behind him. Surely, he thought, whoever might be inside knew there was company *outside*. The sound of the arriving cars, and then his footsteps, would have been easy to hear through the aluminum walls.

Whoever was home, then, was not in any apparent rush to conduct a meet-and-greet.

Grissom went up to the door, standing slightly to its side. This was standard procedure when there was even a hint of the possibility of violence, and Gloria had already proven herself to be of shaky constitution . . . putting it graciously. America was a society of gun toters; everybody thought they were cowboys and cowgirls in the Wild West these days. He was not about to stand directly in front of that door, not about to make an easy target of himself if she got to thinking she was Annie Oakley.

He heard voices through the door now. Several voices, both male and female, one of them sounding like Gloria's.

He knocked, slipping the warrant out of his jacket pocket.

"Mrs. Belcher . . . whoever's inside with you . . . I suggest someone answer immediately," he said in an even voice. "We have a court order that entitles us to enter the premises—"

The door swung open almost immediately, Charlie Belcher staring at him from the inside of the trailer. Wearing a tank-top undershirt and cargo pants, he was unkempt and unshaven, several days' worth of beard shadowing his cheeks, blurring the definition of his mustache.

"What the hell you doin' back again?" Charlie said. He looked at Grissom, then past him at Sara and the uniforms. "How come you got them cops with you?"

Grissom had been doing precisely the same thing as Charlie, only in reverse—taking rapid inventory of what was visible through the doorway. He saw cartons on the floor, some of them shut, others with clothes draped or tumbled about them. He saw a counter with quarrying tools spread out all over its surface—chisels, hammers, reamers, shovels, rock drills, more specialized equipment he couldn't identify. He saw segments of the transportable deck leaning against the wall. He saw a combined kitchenette and dining area with a bluish Formica table in the center and molded plastic stack chairs around it.

An overweight, heavily made-up woman of around thirty sat very still in one of the chairs.

Dressed in a violet tube top and stovepipe jeans, a peroxide blond perm overflowing her shoulders, she was looking out at Grissom with rigid apprehension.

Anything but still on another of the plastic chairs, Gloria Belcher had spun around to face him.

"Get away from here, and take those police with you!" she said. "I already told you once to leave us alone!"

Grissom took a breath. He had guessed this was how things would go with Gloria and found himself wondering if she'd ever made an utterance that wasn't of hostility or spoken at anything less than peak volume.

"Mrs. Belcher, we aren't going anywhere," he said, holding out the official document in his hand now. "I have a warrant issued by the Superior Court giving us authorization to search the premises—"

His sentence was quickly interrupted. Gloria sprang to her feet like a jack-in-the-box, the sudden movement bowling her seat over onto the floor with a crash.

"No," she said. "No, you ain't. You can bring them papers right back where you got 'em? Bring 'em back or shove 'em, hear me?"

Grissom was thinking, yes, he could hear her quite well. It was possible he would go deaf someday, and for that he could thank a genetic abnormality he had inherited from his mother. The surgery he'd had to mitigate and perhaps avert his developing condition seemed to have taken— the loss of hearing he'd experienced some years back was barely noticeable these days. But he was half convinced he would be able to hear Gloria Belcher's rantings even if his cochlea had turned to stone.

He flicked a glance around at the unis, his calm expression letting them know that he was doing all right so far, but that they had better get ready for trouble, just in case.

"Mrs. Belcher, I think you'd better step aside—"

And that was when Gloria propelled herself across the trailer at Grissom, both hands raised and clutching at him, her fingers hooked into claws.

"Filth!" she shouted at him, a look of uncontrolled wrath on her face. "Such vile *filth*—"

"No, please." Charlie had half turned, trying to position himself between them. "She can't—it won't do us any good. She can't . . ."

"Don't you say that to her!" Gloria's eyes were large white circles, her cheeks flushed to an almost bruised purple color. "Don't you dare tell her what to do!"

She lunged around her son, rushing forward with her fingers opening and closing, opening and closing, as if ferociously tearing invisible hunks out of the very air. Grissom had turned to avoid her, but she still managed to wind up almost on top of him as a couple of uniforms came racing past Sara to the trailer, shouldering Grissom aside and then hustling through the door, one of them with his nine-mil drawn from its holster and pointing at Charlie, his partner somehow getting his arms around Gloria, pinning her against the wall with an audible, ugly smack of flesh against metal, and then holding her up against it as the other two officers came in to join them. One of these last cops inside jerked her arms behind her back, restraining them until the other could get her wrists flex-cuffed together.

Grissom was suddenly aware that the woman at the table had stood up at some point during all the uproar and started bawling away, her eyes horrified, her hands flying up to her mouth to stifle her great, hitching sobs.

"Darlene." This was from Charlie, facing her, his voice sorrowful. "Don't cry, I'm gonna take care—"

"Take care a yourself an' forget that whore-woman!" Even with three cops on her, Gloria had wrenched her head around to look at the woman. "She's responsible for all our family's troubles. All of 'em."

Charlie stood there with his face devoid of expression. His shoulders slumped, he seemed almost spent. "Mama . . ."

"They give gifts to all whores," Gloria was shouting with her cheek up against the wall. "To all whores . . ."

Standing behind Grissom and the cluster of police officers, Sara ran her eyes over to Charlie, holding them steadily on him for several seconds.

Watching him closely, closely, before moving on to help Grissom commence with his search.

It was full night when they left the trailer park in Grissom's car, the two police cruisers loaded with evidence from the Belcher family's mobile homes. This included cartons of mining tools that might have been used to render the blunt-force trauma to Adam's head and Charlie and Gloria Belcher's mining boots.

Charlie's boots had been removed from a corner of the double-wide where he had taken them off sometime before. Gloria had been wearing hers. When she repeatedly refused to surrender them, two uniformed officers had been forced to hold her prone on the floor as a third cop struggled to pull them from her feet against her will.

She had screamed, spat, kicked, and thrashed. As the boots were unlaced and removed, she had gnashed her teeth, and the sounds issuing from her mouth had ceased to be intelligible. Foamy saliva had run over her lips and chin.

Watching her behavior, Grissom had related it with concern to a grand-mal seizure and asked Charlie Belcher and the younger woman in the trailer—she had identified herself as Darlene Newell, Charlie's live-in girlfriend—whether either knew if Gloria had a history of epilepsy.

Charlie had insisted she did not and then pleaded with her to calm down.

Grissom had been relieved when she finally subsided.

Now, his high beams streaming out ahead to give him some chance of dodging the road's most hazardous pitfalls, he jounced over miles of ruined blacktop toward the downtown area, where the flood was forgotten and tourists could drive their cars in smoothly restored lanes. In his rearview mirror, he could see the bright circles of the headlights from one of the police cruisers, keeping pace several car lengths back.

To Grissom's right in the passenger seat, Sara stared out into the darkness. She had not spoken a word since they left the trailer court.

She looked drained. It occurred to him that her eyes were staring out the windshield but not see-ing what was in front of them. Her thoughts, too, would be somewhere far away.

"You okay?" he asked.

She gave him a shrug. That was good, Grissom thought. Entire days had gone by when he'd been unable to lift Sara from her reveries.

"Gloria wasn't easy to watch," he said.

She shrugged again. "Just another night with your average squabbling family," she said in a flat voice. "Raving mom calls her son's girlfriend a whore. She's wrestled to the floor so we can tear off her shoes and practically works herself rabid. But the son says it's okay, she gets a little out of control when she's excited, and all's well that ends well. We get what we came for. And maybe it'll help us determine if Adam Belcher was killed by his mother or was a victim of fratricide or if it was a collaborative effort. Or possibly none of the above. Though it sure looks like Mom dumped him in a cave pool." She paused. "It goes on and on and on. And then we march in to sort through the wreckage like the cleanup crews at the Fair-mark golf course."

Grissom considered the last thing she'd said. "Are you only talking about the Belcher case?" he said.

"Yes," she said, then paused and shook her head. "No," she said. "I don't know."

Grissom drove on in silence for a while. "She didn't only call the girlfriend a whore," he said. "Do you recall the specific phrase Gloria used when she went into that tirade about her?"

"Something about giving her gifts," Sara said. "That what you mean?"

"'They give gifts to all whores,'" Grissom said. "It's a quote from the King James Bible. Or part of one. Ezekiel, chapter sixteen, verse thirty-three."

Sara's thoughts seemed to come further out of her mind's own depths. Grissom had been hope-ful they might. He'd wriggled the same kind of baited hook that might draw at them.

"The entire verse is, 'They give gifts to all whores, but thou givest thy gifts to all thy lovers, and hirest them, that they may come unto thee on every side for thy whoredom.'"

Sara looked at him.

"Eidetic memory in action," she said.

Grissom liked that. He had her back. "Ezekiel was one of the latter prophets of the Old Testament," he said. "He lived during the Jewish diaspora in Babylon, and that passage was from a reprimand to Hebrews who'd deviated from traditional practices. He was writing figuratively, comparing their cultural assimilation to an adulteress giving her affections to her lovers. And scolding them for it."

Silence. The car shuddered over a rough grade. Grissom grappled with the steering wheel as it tugged toward the nonexistent road shoulder.

"So was Gloria calling Charlie or Darlene names?" Sara said

"Good question. Maybe both."

Sara's face was thoughtful. "When Charlie was upset, he used the pronoun *she* as a direct form of address to his mother. As if he were talking about a different person."

"I noticed that too," Grissom said. "Gloria stuck with the same form of response. Used the word *her,* third person, referring to herself."

"It fits," Sara mouthed quietly.

"What does?"

She looked out the windshield into the night.

"When I was a kid, one of my foster homes

was in Tulare County, California. A town called Higby," she said. "You have some of the poorest communities in the country there. Farms that can't compete on the market with growers in Peru. No jobs, illiteracy, disenfranchisement. And that leads to frustration, alcoholism, and abuse. It wasn't a fun place, and I was glad I got pulled from it fast."

Grissom glanced at her briefly and drove on without comment.

"I had a girlfriend in school. Her name was Britney. She had a single mom on welfare. It seemed to me that Britney always had a black eye or a split lip. Once she came to school with a broken arm."

"The teachers didn't become suspicious?"

"In those days, they'd say she was accident-prone. It made it easier on them," Sara said. "Maybe things have changed nowadays, I don't know. But I remember going to Britney's house once. We were in her room playing, and her mother came stomping through the door. She was mad or drunk, probably both. And she just went off on Britney. Screaming at her. Throwing her toys around the room. I remember she slapped her across the face for no good reason. I didn't know what to do and just found a corner to hide in and cried." Sara closed her eyes. "Britney kept screaming. 'She's hurting me, she's hurting me.' I didn't know who she was talking about. At first, I thought maybe she was blaming me for something so her mother would stop wailing on her. And then I realized she wasn't talking about me at all."

Grissom considered that a second. "I pick up the psychological journals sometimes," he said.

"Bedtime reading?"

He didn't smile. "There have been articles about the origins of terms of reference. They're complex. But that sounds like a twisted sort of politeness in a dominant-submissive relationship. With associations of power and control for the person being addressed."

Sara nodded. "And who do you think does the controlling in the Belcher clan?" she asked.

"She."

"Yeah."

Grissom was oblivious to rolling over a pothole. Sara braced herself by grabbing on to the top of the dash. A five count later, the patrol car behind them went banging over it.

"Gloria's very powerful in that family dynamic," he said. "She won't talk if we bring her in. As long as he's under her influence, Charlie won't, either. And if they don't, we may never know what happened up at the Belcher quarry."

Sara took a moment to answer him. She appeared to be concentrating.

"I have a hunch about Charlie," she said.

Grissom raised an eyebrow. "How's that?"

"I'm not sure. A hunch is a hunch. It's something about how he acted toward Darlene."

"*Omnia vincit amor*. She presents competition for Mother."

"Maybe." Sara shrugged. "It might be what that whole whore of Babylon rant was about. Or part of it."

"Charlie would have to be removed from Gloria's influence for us to get results," Grissom said. "Talking to them separately wouldn't be enough. She couldn't find out about it."

"I know."

"You think that can be done?"

Sara watched Grissom's brights fan over the crumbled road.

"While you were overseeing the evidence collection, I offered Charlie my business card," she said. "I didn't say anything . . . just held it out and let him choose whether to even acknowledge me."

The car veered a little. This time, it was Grissom's fault. He'd let the wheel slip in his surprise. "And?" he said.

Sara looked at him. "He took it right out of my hand and stuffed it into his pocket," she said. As the car swayed again, she added. "Now, will you please pay attention to your driving before those uniforms pull us over?"

Warrick was snoozing in the break room when the hubbub started.

His exhausting day had begun with an early meeting of the noggins with Catherine about the

Nevada Rose probe. It had been followed by Grissom's decree that he assist Greg Sanders with the flood-pattern CG animation in the *other* Nevada Rose investigation, and later on brought him and Cath to the condominium tower where Eleanor Samuels secretly resided, and where the zillionaire celebs buying up its lavish high-rise apartments like little red Monopoly hotels stacked one atop the other had taken to calling them sky mansions to impress one another and the plebs populating the world below—though Warrick could imagine his Tonte Mavis in New Orleans simply praising them as "bully ol' places." After all that, plus some odds and ends at headquarters to take him through to the early evening, he had found himself stumbling around cross-eyed and dead on his feet.

Retreating to the break room for what he'd figured would be a brief intermission, he'd gotten a ham and American cheese on white and a Gatorade from the vending machines, plopped into a chair, and conked out before he'd even flicked the cap off his drink, let alone peeled the cellophane wrap from his sandwich.

This was right around five-thirty in the evening.

Forty minutes later, Catherine stopped into the room to get a coffee and screw around with Grissom's chess pieces, to find Warrick snoring away with the unopened Gatorade bottle still tucked between his thighs. His sandwich having long since been snatched from his lap by some stealthy food thief, she knew nothing of it. But the sight of him with his head lolling against the back of his chair, his eyes twitching under their lids in deep REM sleep, and his mouth agape had tweaked a merciful impulse in her, and she had quietly left the room, figuring she would give him another half hour or so to rest up.

Not five minutes passed before the outbreak of commotion snapped Warrick from his deep slumber to full, wide-eyed awareness without an instant's transition, causing him to spring from his chair with a startled bound that sent his beverage flying from his lap to the floor, where the bottle would roll under the seat to lie forgotten until a member of the office cleaning staff found it and took it home to her kid, who was heavy into Rollerblading and sports drinks.

Rushing across the room to its entryway now, blinking the glueyness from his eyes, Warrick stuck his head out to see what was going on.

What met his eyes were at least twenty uniformed cops and detectives filling the corridor wall to wall, the group hustling in his direction like a single multiheaded organism. As they came closer, he recognized Vince Millar, Fireball Baker's attorney, hustling along in the middle of the throng, his expression clearly one of intense dismay and agitation.

A heartbeat later, Warrick saw what he'd already assumed must be the reason for the lawyer's unhappiness to his immediate right.

Dressed in a plain blue sweatshirt and brown dress jeans, Fireball Baker was walking briskly toward the examination rooms up the hallway. As Warrick spotted him, it looked as if Baker saw him, too, something that was confirmed moments later when the baseball player halted in midstride to face him outside the break-room door, his mixed escort pulling a short stop around him.

The two men looked at each other, Warrick just inside the doorway, Baker just outside.

"Well," Baker said, "I'm here."

Warrick looked at him and nodded.

"Dave tells me I don't know what I'm getting myself into," Baker said. "Would've liked it better if I stayed home tonight, where those photogs camped out in your parking lot couldn't mob me. I told Dave I didn't do anything to Rose. And that I'd be okay."

Warrick groped for a response. When he finally gave one, it wasn't anything he'd have expected. "How'd your tournament do the other day?" he said.

"Took in over three million dollars for the kids," Baker said. "We were setting our goal at two."

"That's great," Warrick said. "Congrats."

Baker looked at him. "I figure you were my man," he said. "Might've brought me luck after all. It helped me decide to listen to your advice and take those tests."

Warrick once again found himself at a loss for words. Meanwhile, the crowd was stirring restlessly around Baker, and he seemed well aware of it.

"Well," he said, "catch you later."

"Later."

Baker took a step along, hesitated, looked back at Warrick. "Still my man?" he said.

Warrick looked at him steadily and thought back to something Baker had said to him at the golf course. "I'm hoping you won't need to depend on that," he said.

The ballplayer grinned and turned away.

Hanging back in the entry for a while, Warrick watched Baker and the mob around him continue to push on up the hall.

After leaving Warrick dead to the world in the break room, Catherine had brought her coffee back to her office, taken off the lid, and decided to make a phone call before she drank it.

She had been trying to get hold of Dr. Layton Samuels ever since she and Warrick had left the Vista Tower condos, which was now several hours ago. But his office receptionist had said he'd gone home after a surgery that evening—his residence was in the same Seven Hills neighborhood as the Cosmetic Surgery Center and Anti-aging Spa— and Catherine's multiple attempts to reach him there also had failed, yielding one-way conversations with an answering machine.

Still, CSI-3 Willows was nothing if not stubbornly persistent and was hopeful she could get hold of the good doctor and give him a follow-up visit.

She reached for the phone, punched in his number for the third or fourth time, and listened. *Ring, ring, ring,* and his outgoing message came on again.

Catherine frowned. *Okay,* she thought. *Two can play the same game. I'll keep listening to your recorded voice, you'll listen to mine. And we'll see which one of us cracks first.*

"This is Captain Willows from the criminalistics lab again," she said into the phone. "Same message as before. It's absolutely urgent that you return my call as soon as possible. You can contact me at my office at any time—I'll arrange to be paged if I'm out. Thank you very much, Dr. Samuels. I do look forward to hearing from you."

And that was that.

Eyeing her coffee, Catherine was about to rack the receiver when a couple of things happened to her almost simultaneously.

The first was hearing a sudden clamor out in the hallway.

The second was looking toward her open door to see David Phillips, the assistant coroner, framed within it, looking back at her with clipboard in hand.

"Dave," she said. What brings you to the lab?"

"A couple of things about the Nevada Rose

Demille inquiry," he said. "I'm meeting one of the techs on my break and figured I would stop by our office rather than call. Little did I know about the commotion."

Catherine peered past him. "You have any idea what's going on out there—"

"Not what, but 'who'," he said, flinging an imaginary pitch. "The baseball guy's come in for an examination."

"Mark Baker."

Phillips nodded. "I figured you'd know who I meant when I showed you my four-seamer. As opposed to breaking balls, for instance."

Catherine refrained from making a comment. She was thinking Warrick had obviously done a better job of swaying Fireball to cooperate than she had thus far of getting a lousy phone call returned. And she was still wondering about the noise outside.

"Did Baker bring along his whole damn team?"

Dave shrugged. "That pack of reporters in the parking lot tried to mob the guy. So a bunch of uniforms and detectives went out to rescue him."

Catherine looked at Phillips. Why was he standing there in her doorway, anyway?

"So," she said. "What's up?"

"Couple things about the Nevada Rose Demille inquiry," he said. "Got a minute?"

She waved him in.

"By the way, before we get to this," he said, tapping his clipboard, "was that Dr. Layton Samuels I heard you talking to on the phone?"

"Actually, I was having a limited communication with his answering machine," she said. And then realized she'd never told him about Samuels's connection to Rose Demille. Or, in fact, discussed the case with him at all since the day the body was discovered. "Why do you ask?"

"Nothing having to do with anything," he said. "Well, you know, I was curious. On a personal level. Considering his reputation."

Catherine gave him a bemused glance. "You thinking of having plastic surgery?" she said.

He shook his head. "Why mess with perfection? My wife says I'm an Adonis."

"And who would ever doubt her?"

"Ha-ha," he said. "But you know, seriously, Samuels is a pioneer. Going back."

Catherine looked at him. "How far?"

"Like back to when I was a kid," he said. "He was the first plastic surgeon to use the drug succinylcholine."

Catherine dug in her memory for knowledge of it. Found zip. Well, except . . . "Choline's what they put in vitamin B complex, isn't it?" she said.

"Right," Dave said. "It affects the neurotransmitters. On its own, it helps with memory, cognition, even heart function. But *succinyl*choline's a different animal."

"That being?"

"Synthetic curare," Phillips said. "Curare really being a kind of blanket name for a whole bunch of natural neuromuscular blocking agents. The thing about the drug is that it works fast. Back in the 'seventies, it had the shortest duration of all muscle relaxants. Doesn't put patients out for too long, because it starts breaking down into its chemical ingredients once it's in the system."

"And that's a good thing?"

"In plastic surgery," Phillips said. "When they perform rhinoplasties—"

"Nose jobs."

"Right, sorry for the medicalese. When you do a nose job, it's desirable for a patient to remain semiconscious and recover quickly from anesthesia. There's a lot of blood running down the throat, and it's better to have the swallow reflex going so there's less chance of choking."

Catherine thought about that a second. "Short version . . . what are the drug's specific effects?"

"Basically, it brings on short-term muscular paralysis," Phillips said.

"And the danger of overdose? If any?"

"Well . . . I suppose because it relaxes the chest and abdominal muscles, the drug could impair respiration and heart activity, even lead to asphyxia—"

He abruptly stopped talking, his mouth opening and closing as if he'd been suddenly rendered mute.

Catherine looked at him, her mind racing. "What is it?" she said.

"Catherine," he said, "were you talking to Dr. Samuels in connection to the Nevada Rose case?"

She nodded briskly in the affirmative.

"Wow, jeez, " Dave said.

"Wow, jeez *what*, for God's sake?" she said. "Dave, will you quit keeping me in suspense?"

He fingered the top sheet of paper on his clipboard again. "I was putting fresh toe tags on the body—"

"Rose Demille's?"

"Right, Rose Demille . . . the first set of tags got smudged up during the initial autopsy, and I like to keep them legible."

"And?"

"And I noticed tiny needle marks between the fourth and fifth toes of her left foot," Phillips said.

Catherine straightened in her chair. "You show them to Robbins?"

"Yeah."

"And?"

"He told me to let you know about it," Phillips said. "And said he was following through."

Catherine sat facing him, her thoughts still speeding along.

"Say succinylcholine was injected into Rose Demille after she was tied up and gagged . . ."

"It would have put her in an almost immediate state of muscular paralysis."

"And left her that way long enough for someone to have burked her?"

"Definitely could have," Phillips said. "And the thing is, you wouldn't detect it with the usual toxicological batteries."

"Why's that?"

"Like I said, it metabolizes at a rapid rate. Succinic acid and choline are chemicals normally found in the human body. That's why you find them in all those natural vitamin supplements. The breakdown levels in the bloodstream were probably so unexceptional the tox lab didn't chart them."

Catherine studied him carefully. "There's a *but*," she said. "Give it to me."

"If she was injected with succinylcholine and we conduct a fresh battery of tests on her brain, it's likely its components will show higher-than-normal levels. Since the drug's an alkaloid, it's absorbed by neurotransmitters and builds up there."

All at once, Catherine found herself thinking about the death of Eleanor Samuels's first husband.

"Tell Robbins I'm looking into a connection between Samuels and Rose Demille," she said. "And that we need to get those tests done right away."

Phillips nodded but didn't move an inch from where he was standing in front of her desk.

"Was there anything else?" She wished she could teleport him back to the morgue with a glance. The information he'd just reported was too damned important for her to want to lose a minute.

Dave looked down at his clipboard. "Remember that empty pill organizer that was in Rose's dresser drawer?"

Catherine nodded.

"We found minute traces of Verapamil and lithium in it," Dave said. "That's probably incidental, no big deal. My guess is Rose may have suffered from migraines at some point. It's a pretty common problem, and those drugs would be used in combination for first-line treatment."

"First line?" Catherine was unfamiliar with the term.

"Depending on a patient's responsiveness to migraine therapy, doctors go from first-line to second-line to third-line designations," he said. "First-line works for most people with moderate occurrences. Lots of times, the condition clears up, and that's that. But if you have to go third-line, it means the patient's having a severe, persistent problem and that nothing else has helped." He paused. "At that stage, you'd use stronger drugs . . . I've even heard of liquid cocaine nasal drops being used to ameliorate the pain in severe cases. But it'd be very rare."

Catherine was recalling Doc Robbins's summary of the tox findings during the autopsy. "There were no traces of those substances—Verapamil and lithium—in Rose's body," she said.

"Right." Phillips nodded again. "So what's in the pill dispenser's probably incidental. The drugs didn't contribute to her death."

"Thanks for the rundown, Adonis," she said with a wink.

Phillips gave a small, shy smile. "Some people around here think you're quite an Aphrodite yourself," he said, and spun around on his heels to exit the office hastily.

9

KYLE GIBBONS SAT in the antique wing chair with a cognac, using his remote to browse through the channels on the large flat-panel TV screen in front of him, trying to decide what would be the lesser of two horrible evils. He wasn't much of a drinker—or a television watcher, come to think. He liked doing physical things, working up a healthy sweat. That was apart from what he did for a living, maybe the reason he'd taken a life-long hobby and turned it into a profession. Having grown up in northern Massachusetts, where it was freezer-cold outside for half the year, too cold to do anything but stay cooped up indoors, he'd fallen in love with the warm climate here in Nevada.

Even now, after dark, he would have rather been outdoors. In the pool or maybe on the jogging track or the lighted basketball court.

It was what they would do together sometimes—or had done until recently—shooting
hoops, going one-on-one. More times than not,
Mark had him beat. What the hell, though. It
didn't matter what kind of shape he himself was
in. He'd helped Mark these past few years, no
doubt about it. Worked out a torturously extreme
fitness routine that had enabled him to adjust to
the wear and tear that came from pushing his body
to the max and beyond for almost two decades.

But Mark was almost forty, and baseball years
were like goddamned dog years. Half the kids he
faced whenever he climbed up on the mound
were thinking they were going to knock the old
guy's fastball way out of the stadium and then
get back into the clubhouse and text their friends
back home that they'd launched one off the leg-
endary Fireball Baker. But they learned. They
learned how he'd gotten where he was. Learned
what made him *who* he was and still allowed him
to perform at a certain level, compete with guys
practically young enough to be his kids.

There was the work. The training regime. Sure,
Gibbons set the goals and could keep pace. But
beat him?

Mark was the professional athlete. The peren-
nial all-star. He'd been a winner his entire life.
Had busted his tail to stay a winner.

Gibbons was ten years younger than Mark
but had never once felt he had what it took to be
anything like him.

He sipped his Courvoisier and found himself back on that damned gossip channel. *Entertainment 24.* Your fucking 'round-the-clock ghoul fest. Tune in any hour of the night or day and see people eaten alive by smiling hosts and pop-psych talking heads waiting for the next celebrity sex scandal, child-custody suit, DUI incident, check-in or checkout from a detox center—or if they got really lucky, a fatal overdose.

When it came to dead celebrities, nothing topped a murder, though. They could bundle together a whole lot of juicy material with a murder. The rumors, allegations, investigations, arrest footage, and trial coverage. The so-called friends coming out of the woodwork with their personal recollections. With the resources at their disposal, it was endless. They could roll over every stone, pull up video footage going back decades. *Here's the suspect in his party days. Here's the victim looking sexy. Here they are together, the beautiful couple in happier times.*

Murder was the whole lively package for them.

Those cannibals.

Those grinning cannibals.

They'd cornered Mark tonight, gotten exactly what they wanted. He had decided to handle things the way he always did, straight up, no compromises. Walk on into that police laboratory and take the tests they wanted him to take. Poke him, prod him, stick their DNA swabs in his mouth, take fingerprints, his blood, make him piss into a cup—whatever they wanted. He'd said he would look them in their eyes and answer all their questions with their video cameras running, give them a written statement, stick his initials on every page, every sentence of every page.

Almost forty years old, and Mark could still throw a fastball that lit up the radar guns, blow it right past those swaggering young kids who thought they could make their bones off him, wind up on a highlight reel. *There I am, Mom, that's me blasting one of Mark Baker's heaters three hundred feet over the outfield wall. That's me you see beating the best.*

But Mark refused to be beaten. The reporters for the newspapers, magazines, and Web sites would write about his conditioning, his dedication to routine. That was what Gibbons had helped with.

Except it was his will that made him what he was.

His will and his guts.

They were the ingredients you couldn't get from workouts. You either had them or you didn't.

Mark Baker told Gibbons he had never backed down from anything or anyone in his life and was not going to start now. As if Gibbons had needed to hear it from him. As if he didn't know him well enough after all these years together. As if he'd even think he could change his mind about it. Right afterward, Mark had called Dave Millar and told him to meet him over at the police headquarters, that he was driving in right away. And when Millar started screaming at him about it, he'd told the lawyer he could either go along with the program or walk away, but he wasn't changing his mind. He was leaving the house in ten minutes, see you later or not.

Listening to the phone call, Gibbons had accepted that his going in was a foregone conclusion. He knew Baker better than anyone and had gotten behind his decision right away.

Mark Baker hadn't killed Nevada Rose Demille. Couldn't possibly have killed her.

The question was . . . could he prove his innocence without giving up the one thing he would rather spend his life behind bars than reveal?

Gibbons's doubts had been eating away at him even before he put on the TV and saw that those people with their cameras had been camped out, waiting outside in the parking lot of the crime lab.

Those cannibals, those fucking human piranha.

They'd swarmed him the minute he got out of his car, gotten right in his face, chased him to the building. It was as if he'd had to push through a bristling jungle of cameras and microphones with those fuzzy goddamned windscreens.

And now here it was on national television, on *Entertainment 24*, the footage delivered and edited and framed with recaps from the ghouls even before prime time. Here it was in crisp high definition, Mark Baker being swarmed by the fucking flesh eaters for everyone to hang back and watch in the comfort of their living rooms. There wasn't much, maybe two or three minutes, but the flesh eaters had spliced it together twenty different ways so they could show it again and again and again.

"*Fireball, are you able to confirm Rose Demille's maid found a gym bag on the lawn . . . ?*"

"*. . . that you've been issued a subpoena by the district attorney . . . ?*"

"*. . . decided to confess . . . ?*"

"*. . . sadomasochistic strangulation . . . ?*"

"*. . . are ready to plead to a lesser charge in exchange for . . . ?*"

Though he wished he'd thought of it earlier, Gibbons had gotten the idea to call ahead and notify the police that Mark was on his way. So they could come out and escort him into the place, let him hang on to some little remaining bit of his of privacy and dignity. The reporters had worked out some kind of arrangement with the cops, or the city, or whatever, that allowed them to lurk in ambush out there in the parking lot, but entering the premises was another story. Once the cops came and assembled around Mark to bring him into the building, the flesh eaters and their mikes and camera lenses had gotten boxed out.

But still . . . still, they'd gotten what they needed for their nightly programming loop. They always managed to sink their fangs in for one or two painful, bloody bites.

Always.

Gibbons set his drink down and massaged his brow. He couldn't watch any more of it. He needed to get out, work off some tension, maybe run some laps. Vegas . . . if you didn't mind the heat, you always had the weather on your side.

The odds, though, were something else, and Gibbons was afraid—scared out of his wits, in fact—that they were piling up on Mark Baker by the minute.

Piling up high and deep enough to bury him forever.

Surrounded by tall piles of overstuffed cartons and other loose odds and ends removed from the Belcher trailer homes, Sara Sidle stood in the crime lab's evidence storage room looking beleaguered and thinking she would desperately need to corral some obedient junior tech—at least one—to help log all the junk in.

Her preoccupation with the repetitive but exacting work had helped her shake off the downer she'd been thrown into watching Gloria Belcher's uncontrolled flare-up of cuckooness. It was Grissom, too. Gris always somehow dispelled the gluey darkness when it threatened to suck her under. But the work—the nuts and bolts of it— that was always good for her. It took her mind off the past, allowed her to concentrate on what was pressing and tangible.

She had already spent the better part of two hours getting a very significant head start with what were likely the key evidentiary items. These included Charlie and Gloria's work boots (made of premium leather, of course), the quarrying tools from Charlie's double-wide, and various articles of clothing from both trailers. But Gloria Belcher had made it impossible to be picky as far as conducting the seizure. With two of the cops who'd accompanied Sara and Grissom to the Sunderland Trailer Court busy just keeping her from bouncing off the walls, it was unanimously decided to grab whatever stood even a remote chance of having some forensic investigative value—which had translated into everything in sight that wasn't nailed down.

And so here Sara was, all alone in the temporary storage room, really figuring she would need to scare up a tech. Even with help, she guessed it was a sure thing the sorting, bagging, and tagging would take all night. Practical remedy for her funk or not, she did not intend to be at it until she was old and gray. Maybe, Sara thought, she would nab somebody from among the large group roaming around the building in starstruck efforts to catch glimpses of the famous baseball hero involved in Catherine and Warrick's burking case. It would serve those whippersnappers right.

Sara was turning toward the door when her cell phone vibrated in her blazer's inside pocket. She saw that the call, a blocked number, had been forwarded from her office line.

This was not anything she deemed worthy of a second thought. Sara kept her call-forwarding option engaged whenever she was out of the office. Furthermore, the majority of LVPD employees, from law-enforcement personnel to clerks, were understandably—some would say obsessively—wary of having their numbers get out to strangers and therefore blocked the caller-ID feature as a general practice. When your job description involved constant interaction with hardened criminals and crazies of every ilk, you tended to be very cautious about releasing your personal information.

She flipped open the phone and raised it to her ear.

"Hi," she said. "This is Sara . . ."

"You told me to call," said a voice at the other end.

She instantly recognized it, and felt the skin prickle at the back of her neck. "Charlie?"

"I'm in my truck," he said.

"In your truck where?"

"You asked me to call," he said. "So I am."

She felt her stomach knot. That was not an answer to her question. His disjointedness troubled her.

She tried again. "Charlie . . . where are you?"

"I told you." His voice was trembling. "I'm in the truck. On my cell."

Calm, Sara thought. *Stay calm.* Charlie sounded agitated. It would do no good at all if he picked up anything similar in her.

"Where are you going?" she said, wishing she had time to patch Grissom into this call. Positive Grissom could handle him. That he would know exactly what to say. But she did not have time, she was on her own. It was up to her to know what to do here.

And then a thought struck her. Rammed into her brain so absolutely that she almost slapped her forehead, wondering how it hadn't come to her sooner.

"Are you heading over here, Charlie?" she said. "Are you coming to see me?"

"Yeah. I got the address. It's on that card. The one you stuck in my hand."

All right, Sara thought. *All right, we're making progress.*

"Charlie, I'm very glad to hear it," she said. "I'm right here waiting for you—"

"I killed my brother," Charlie said, cutting her off.

Sara took a deep breath. How to respond to that? *How?*

"Charlie, listen to me. You'll have to tell me all this when we're together. You can stay on the phone now, keep talking to me right now, because I'm here for you and want to make sure

I understand everything you say. But for me to help you . . . I need you here with me."

A sound escaped him, a kind of choked-off whimper. "It was all about that gemstone," he said. "The Nevada Rose. But it wasn't all my fault. Part of the blame was his. You got to put some of it on him."

Sara was silent. She didn't want to interrupt. Let him have his space.

"Me and Adam, we was gonna to sell it to that Smithsonian museum in Washington," Charlie said. "I didn't want to. I thought there was other ways we could get more for it. But we got sick of arguin' back and forth about it. Sicker of bein' broke. And so I told my brother to go ahead an' do it . . . to go ahead an' cut the deal."

"And is that what you did?"

Silence.

"Charlie . . ."

"It was gonna be a fifty-fifty split," he said in a breaking voice. "That's what we agreed to. Half for me, half for him. That sounds fair, don't it, Miss Sidle?"

Long, deep breath, she thought. *Innnnnn . . . then out.* "Yes, Charlie," she said. "It sounds fair."

"So then, why would anybody want to change it?"

"Is that what happened, Charlie?"

He didn't say anything. Sara waited. Nothing.

"Charlie, go on . . ."

More nothing. No . . . not nothing. He was

weeping now. Weeping outright into the phone.

She suddenly became terrified she would lose him. "I'm still listening, Charlie. Tell me what happened."

"It got changed," he said with a hitching sob. "Right before the people from the museum came to pick up the stone, it got changed. Adam . . . he . . . he showed up while I was at our mine camp, wanting to make the percentage sixty-forty. His favor. An' you can figure what happened."

Sara wasn't sure how to reply. She did not want to put words in his mouth, do anything to color his admission.

"What happened, Charlie?" she decided to say after a moment. "Tell me what happened at the camp."

"We got into a fight. A goddam *brawl*'s what it was. Adam hit his head—must've been on a rock, I don't know—and then the next thing . . . next thing, he ain't breathin'. Adam's dead, an' I don't know what to do . . . and I drug him in that pool where the rain comes through the adit. *I drug my brother in that stinking, filthy pool to rot—*"

Charlie broke off, crying harder now.

Sara wondered how he could possibly drive in that state. She was thinking he was going to pieces on her, was bound get into some kind of accident on the road if he didn't somehow pull out of it.

"Charlie, I . . . look, how far are you from me right now?"

"Few minutes," he rasped. "Five, ten."

"Good, Charlie. That's really great."

"You gonna wait for me, right?"

"I promised you I would, Charlie. I'm not going anywhere till I see you—"

There was momentary dead air on the phone. Sara prayed to a God she'd never trusted that it wasn't a drop-off.

"Charlie, you there?"

More of that dull no-sound.

"Charlie—"

And then he was back. "I'm sorry," he said.

"What?"

Another burst of sobs. And then a horrendous semi-articulate moan: *"Sorryyeeeeahhhhhhh."*

"Charlie!"

The line went silent again. Stayed silent.

Sara's heart pounded against her rib cage.

The call hadn't dropped off that first time. How the hell could she have made such a dumb mistake?

When you get an incoming call-waiting beep at your end of the line, it gives the person at the other end a flat silence. Exactly the sort she had gotten.

Charlie had heard the beep, taken another call, and put her on hold. That was what had happened, Sara was sure of it. Just as she had a gut certainty about who had phoned him.

She went running out of the room as fast as her feet would carry her.

Sara went racing into Grissom's office less than a minute later, grateful to find him there. Winded but too adrenaline-hyped to sit down, she paced in front of his desk and recapped her exchange with Charlie Belcher.

Grissom was quiet for a while as she finished, his expression thoughtful as he looked at her through his eyeglasses.

"Do you believe his confession?" he asked.

"It runs contrary to whatever evidence we've got," Sara said breathlessly. "The only shoe-prints we have got going to that drip pool are Gloria's."

"You've compared the photos from inside the cave with her boots?"

"First thing when we got back here from the trailer court . . . before I even thought about logging in the other evidence."

"And?"

"The size and sole patterns are a precise match."

Grissom thought another moment. "Charlie didn't say anything to you about using a cart or wheelbarrow?"

"No," Sara said. "He said he dragged him. Not once but twice."

Grissom pushed his glasses down the bridge of his nose. Then up again. "Charlie's a large man," he said. "What would you estimate he weighs, two hundred, two hundred and fifty pounds?"

Sara nodded. "He wouldn't have needed to wheel Adam to the pool," she said. "Not those few feet from where the footprints start in that recess."

"But it *looks* like he was wheeled."

"Right."

"Not dragged."

"Right."

"Which is more likely how *Gloria* would have moved him, being about half Charlie's size."

"I know Charlie was lying to me," Sara said. "And I *think* he was covering up for his mother."

"To protect her."

"Yeah."

Grissom's eyebrows drew together. "So," he said, "why did he abruptly end his phone call to you? And more important . . . where is he?"

Sara paced the room with her hands behind her back. Two steps left, two right, two left again, as Grissom watched her intently.

Then she suddenly stopped and stood looking at him across the middle of his desk.

"I don't know what's going on," she said. "I've got an all-points out on the pickup I saw at the trailer court. But I think we'd better head back over there."

Grissom rose from his desk without questioning her. Socrates might have frowned. But it showed why he had won Sara's heart. "I'll put somebody at the front door just in case Belcher shows. And get some uniforms to come with us," he said.

It was almost ten o'clock at night as Warrick stood leaning against the wall a few feet down the corridor from Catherine's office, arms crossed, waiting for her to get off the phone with a detective in New York City who had pledged to expedite her procurement of death records for Eleanor Samuels's first husband—and Layton Samuels's former partner—Dr. Carl Melvoy. According to the obit Warrick had pulled up on the electronic newspaper archive, Melvoy had lived and died on Manhattan's Upper East Side.

The crime lab was quiet now. Fireball Baker had gone home hours ago, leaving behind his biological samples and a somewhat thinned-out group of reporters still garrisoned in the parking lot. Grissom and Sara had left in a hurry soon afterward, heading off on some sort of emergency having to do with the Green Man affair. In short, nothing much was happening.

All Warrick could do for the moment was hang out until Catherine got off the horn with the NYPD, after which the two of them planned to head out to Vista Towers for another talk with Mrs. Samuels, during which they would confront her with some new and very interesting tidbits of information Cath had acquired thanks to Super Dave's penchant for sanitary, unsoiled toe tags on the bodies in his morgue room.

Restless, Warrick strode over to the water cooler, filled a Dixie cup, drained it, and then crunched it into a ball in his hand. He'd just backed up to hook it into the wastebasket with a midrange jump shot, when he saw a guy he didn't recognize out of the corner of his eye, heading up the corridor from the general vicinity of the reception desk, accompanied by one of the uniformed cops who manned the front desk.

Dressed in an eggshell sport coat, brown trousers, and loafers, the civilian was maybe thirty or thirty-five years old, brown-haired, fit-looking, and walking alongside the cop with what seemed to be a very purposeful stride.

Warrick stood near the cooler and watched them, mainly because he was bored senseless and there wasn't much else around to grab his attention. Then, as the pair approached, it suddenly dawned on him that *he* might very well be the reason for their unexpected presence.

As they reached Warrick, the cop stopped and nodded toward the brown-haired guy. "Got somebody here wants to see you," he said, confirming Warrick's assumption that he was indeed why these men were now sharing the hallway with him. "Says it's urgent."

Warrick looked at the guy in the sport coat, saw that he had an adhesive visitor's pass on his breast pocket.

He took in the name on the pass at a glance. *Kyle Gibbons.*

It sounded familiar. Then he remembered when he'd heard it before.

"You're . . . Mark Baker's trainer, right?" he said, thinking Baker had mentioned he'd had a regular workout with him the Sunday after his birthday party at Club Random. And that he'd actually been meaning to give him a call.

The guy had extended his hand. "Good to meet you, Mr. Brown," he said. "Fireball told me you'd talked to him at the golf tournament."

Warrick nodded at him, and they shook, Gibbons looking firmly at Warrick, Warrick returning the look, sizing the trainer up there in the hall, wondering what his reason might be for coming to see him at this relatively late hour of the night.

His eyes still on Warrick, Gibbons said, "Is there a place we can talk? In private, if you don't mind."

Warrick nodded, increasingly eager to find out what the guy might want from him. He would just have to stick his head into Cath's door, tell her that something had come up and he'd need a few minutes. Not that he had any reason to believe those New York badges would rush to get anything done for her over the phone in the next few minutes.

After thanking the cop for bringing Gibbons over, he motioned down the corridor to his office cubicle.

"Sure, there's a place," he said. "Follow me."

There was a large crowd gathered in front of Charlie Belcher's mobile home when Grissom and Sara pulled up to it at a little past ten o'clock, their police accompaniment right on their tail, jamming their brakes down hard so as not to crash into one another's bumpers. *At least* fifteen, twenty residents of the trailer court, by Sara's quick estimate. They were in shorts and T-shirts and robes, in socks or slippers or, in some cases, barefoot, looking shocked and confused, as if they had rushed out of their places and left their lights and televisions on, left their snacks and late suppers and beers sitting on tables and nightstands, left the kids back in their beds with orders to stay put—in short, looking as if they'd abruptly stopped whatever they were doing to come running out to Unit 24, where—as the CSIs and uniforms would later find out—they had heard the awful racket.

The screaming, the crashing, and the gunshots.

Sara looked out at the Belcher trailer. The lights were on inside. It appeared as if every *single* light in the place was on. Brightness leached out between the slats and frames of the window shutters. Brightness spilled from the partly open front door.

Sara wasn't sure why, but she found the stark radiance pouring out of the place into the darkness of night deeply, viscerally disturbing.

She turned toward Grissom, her face taut with worry and dismay. "Gris," she said. Swallowing dryly. "What do we do here?"

He sat thinking a moment, glanced in his

rearview. Behind him, the cops were out of their cruisers now, talking to the people who'd come dashing out of their homes when they heard all the noise, wanting to see what the hell was going on at Charlie Belcher's place.

"Let's wait a minute," he said, shifting around to face her from behind the steering wheel. "See what information they get out of those peop—"

Sara grabbed his forearm, staring out the windshield. Straight out the windshield at the trailer, her mouth dropping wide open. "Gris," she said, nodding in the trailer's direction.

He turned, looked, Sara's fingers still clamped around him, digging hard into his arm.

The trailer's front door, ajar a moment ago, had been flung wide. And standing there inside the entry, bathed in the light streaming through the entry, all that light coming from what had to be every bulb in the place, was Charlie Belcher.

Covered in blood, he was holding a gun to his head. A revolver—Sara thought it was a .38-caliber but couldn't be positive. Between the blinding glare inside the trailer and the blackness outside, she couldn't get her eyes to adjust, and it was tough to see for sure.

Not that it made a difference what kind of gun it was. If it was loaded, and Charlie Belcher pulled the trigger with its barrel pressed against the side of his head, the end result would be the same.

Sara swallowed without moisture again.

The blood all over Charlie—splattering his face, shirt, and pants—gave her a powerful reason to believe that the gun was damned well loaded.

A moment passed. Sara's heart knocked. She shifted around to glance out the rear window, saw two of the cops who'd tagged along from headquarters crouched behind the open driver and passenger doors of their cruiser, their own pistols out. Behind that first patrol car, the other pair of unis was busy handling the crowd of bystanders, clearing them from the scene.

Sara faced the trailer again. Charlie stood there, bloodied from head to toe, the gun barrel pressed to his temple.

Suddenly, she let go of Gris with one hand, her other lunging for her door handle.

"Sara," he said at once. Grabbing *her* arm now. "What are you doing?"

Her head whipped around in his direction. "Going out," she said.

He kept his eyes on her. "No."

"Gris—"

"You can't do it."

"The police have him covered," she said. "They've got two guns on him."

"They can have ten guns, twenty, all he needs is time to fire his at you once," Grissom said, and shook his head. "I won't let you out of this car, Sara. I mean it."

They looked at each other for a moment in silence, Grissom's hand locked around Sara's left arm, her right hand on the handle of the passenger door.

"Please, Charlie won't hurt me," she said.

"You don't know that."

"Yes, I do," Sara said, and as he began shaking his head again she released the door handle and gently, softly placed a hand on his cheek.

"Sara—"

"I know, he won't, trust me," she said. And smiled. "Gris, what do you see?"

Another moment passed.Their eyes still connecting. The two of them joined by their gazes there in the closeness of the car.

And then Grissom let go of her arm, and she turned back toward her door and got out of the car.

"Charlie," Sara said, standing outside the car now. "Put the gun down."

He stood in the doorway facing her, the revolver not moving from his head.

"She killed Darlene," he said. Angling his head back toward the inside of the trailer. "Shot her with this gun. *Shot* her."

Sara looked at Charlie. Sensing the police crouched behind their open cruiser doors behind her, their guns trained on him.

"It won't help if you die, too," she said. "It won't help Darlene or anyone else."

Charlie opened his mouth, closed it, his eyes bright in his blood-smeared face.

"Was her that killed Adam," Charlie said. "I was gonna take the blame. But it was her."

Sara inhaled, exhaled. "Gloria," she said. "Your mother."

He made a snorting sound. "My *mother*," he said. It came out sounding like a curse. "She . . . she tried to meddle with the museum deal, said me an' her ought to get a bigger share of the cash for the Nevada Rose. Claimed I'd done more 'a the work than Adam and deserved more a the profits. But I didn't . . . I knew I didn't . . ." His voice faded.

"Charlie, listen," Sara said. "It would be better if you tell me this after you put away the gun."

"No," he said.

Another deep inhalation. "Charlie, I'm listening to you, I really am," she said. "But the gun—"

"She always told me I was the son that loved her the most," he said, breaking in. "Who'd take care a her when she was old. An' then when you an' your friend showed up askin' questions . . . when that happened, she blamed it on Darlene. For no reason." He paused, sucked in a breath. "She said that Darlene informed on her. Led you to our doorstep. That Darlene was plannin' to take me and the Nevada Rose away from her an' that we'd leave her to fend for herself in the world."

"It wasn't true," Sara said. "You know it, and I know it. You can't blame yourself."

"Who *else* am I supposed to blame?" he said,

keeping the revolver where it was against his head. That damned revolver against his head. "If I'd been at the camp when she confronted Adam, I could've stopped her from smashing him with that rock. If I'd been here when she came after Darlene tonight, accusin' her, tossin' things all over the trailer, threatenin' her with this gun . . . if I'd been here when Darlene called me for help instead a drivin' out to see you . . . make up a lie to protect her . . . spare her from gettin' blamed for what she did to Adam . . . if I'd been *here*—"

He broke off, his voice clogging up, tears flowing from his eyes, mixing with the blood on his cheeks as they flowed down his face.

Sara suddenly remembered the dead air on her phone when he'd called from his truck. The brief call-waiting lull. It had been Darlene contacting Charlie, she thought. Darlene phoning to tell him that Gloria was flying into one of her rages, asking him to come defuse it. And Charlie had changed his plans about confessing, doubled back around to head for home . . .

And arrived there too late.

"Charlie, I think you trust me," Sara said. "Is that right?"

He nodded slowly, crying. "I killed her," he said. "Pulled the gun out of her hand an' killed her."

"I don't want to talk about that," she said. "I just want to talk about you now. You can't take on the guilt for your mother going out of control. For what she did—"

"She killed Adam," he said. "And Darlene."

Raising his voice to a near shriek.

Pushing the gun barrel against his temple with such force it made his head tilt sideways.

"Charlie—"

"She goddamned killed us all . . ."

"Charlie—"

The roar of his pistol as he fired it point-blank against his temple cut her short.

Moments later, rushing into the trailer behind the police, Sara and Grissom found the bodies of Gloria Belcher and Darlene Newell.

It was not a pretty sight. But then, Sara thought, time after time, night after night on the job, the only constant was that they never were.

10

"LOVERS," CATHERINE WILLOWS said, thoughtfully tapping her lip with a pencil. "Fireball Baker and his trainer."

"Gibbons, yeah." Warrick gave a nod from where he sat across her desk. "They've been in a monogamous relationship for a few years now. Three, four, something like that."

Catherine tapped her lip some more. It was now almost ten-thirty, getting along into the night, and she still wanted to make it over to Vista Towers before Eleanor Samuels tucked herself under the covers. Nevertheless, Warrick's account of his conversation with Kyle Gibbons had her nailed to her chair.

"And Baker's affair with Rose Demille?"

"Nothing but a sham," he said. "Or to put it another way, his latest attempt to conceal his homosexuality by being seen in the company of beautiful, sexy women."

"Some way for a person to have to live," she said.

"What else could Baker do?" Warrick replied. "An athlete of his status—a famous *baseball player*—for him to be revealed as gay would be a disaster in his macho world."

"Therefore his photo-op sightings with Rose . . ."

" . . . their public carrying on . . ."

"And the tens of thousands of dollars Baker paid Rose to be his cover," Catherine said. "It took a lot of courage for Gibbons to come see you tonight."

"Yeah."

"And love, too."

"Yup. The guy put everything on the line," he said. "He knew that if Baker found out he'd taken things into his own hands and opened up to us about their secret—*and* if we decided to go public—it'd probably mean the end of their relationship."

"Because Fireball would feel betrayed."

"Yeah," Warrick said. "Wouldn't you?"

Catherine mulled that over, holding the pencil eraser against her lip. "Can't decide," she said. "It's hard for me to relate."

"To being in the closet?"

"To hiding my lifestyle from people or worrying about being judged," she said. "I suppose it's just something I've never done."

Warrick chewed on that a bit, grunted. "Makes me think of something Gibbons said when we got into my office," he said.

"Which was?"

"That it was better for Baker to face the consequences of the truth than go to prison for living a lie," he said. "I didn't follow him at first . . . I mean, that was before he told me about the two of them."

Catherine glanced at the clock. They would have to get going any minute now.

"So the night of Fireball's party, he left Club Random, dropped off Rose, and went straight home just like he claimed," she said.

"Only not for the *reason* he claimed," Warrick said.

"That he had a workout scheduled for the next morning."

"Yup."

Catherine got his meaning. She sighed, slipped her pencil back into its holder, and rose from behind her desk.

The night after the party, when Baker's public charade with Rose Demille concluded, he had hurried home to be with Gibbons so they could celebrate their secret love together.

Eleanor Samuels's apartment in the stratospheric heights above the city. Eleven o'clock at night. Eleanor sitting on her plush red living-room sofa, Catherine and Warrick alongside her in the very spots they had occupied during their last visit.

Her face scrubbed for bed, hair pulled loosely back in a ponytail, Eleanor was wearing a citron yellow silk kimono that closely matched the color of the cactus blooms on the large Georgia O'Keeffe opposite them.

"It could be a coincidence," Eleanor was saying in response to what Catherine had just told her. Her right leg crossed over her left knee under the flap of the kimono. "I don't see how you come here at this hour with these accusations . . ."

"Mrs. Samuels, we're not making accusations," Catherine said.

"Well, whatever you want to call it," she said. "Come here drawing *conclusions*, then . . ."

Catherine looked at her. "Your husband developed and pioneered the use of succinylcholine," she said. "After noticing hypodermic syringe marks between Rose Demille's toes, where they would be very difficult to notice, the coroner re-examined tissue samples from Rose's brain tonight and found unusually high concentrations of the drug's breakdown products."

Eleanor just stared at her. "I don't know what you want from me," she finally said, sighing. "You should be talking to Layton, if anyone, about this. I'm not the one who was having an affair." She shifted against the backrest of the couch. "Besides, say what you will about my husband, it's absurd to suggest he would kill that woman."

"She really had him hooked," Warrick said.

Eleanor shot him a look."What is that supposed to mean?"

"You tell us," he said. "Those were your words when were here just a few hours ago. You said he was hooked, said they were soul mates . . ."

"I believe I also said Layton seemed to accept Rose Demille's . . . *appreciation*, shall we say, for other men." Eleanor's lips tightened at the corners. "Especially those closer to her age."

The CSIs were quiet a moment, Catherine thinking it was time to pull out the stops.

"Mrs. Samuels," she said, "we happened to come across some information about your first husband while conducting routine background checks."

Eleanor looked at her, sitting up very quickly. "Why bring Carl into this conversation?" she said. "What does he have to do with anything that's gone on here?"

"At first, I thought it was nothing much," said Catherine. "But then I found some discrepancies about the reason for his death."

"Reason? What are you talking about?"

Catherine looked at Eleanor unwaveringly now. "The newspaper obituary said he passed away of a heart attack," she said. "But when I contacted the New York Police Department earlier tonight and was able to obtain his official death records, it turns out he died from positional asphyxia. Oddly enough, the same thing that was determined to be what killed Rose De-mille."

Eleanor stared at her. "I thought you weren't accusing me of anything," she said. "But if you're suggesting I knew anything about it . . ."

"Anything about what?"

Eleanor was silent.

"About what?" Catherine repeated.

Several more ticks of silence. Then Eleanor said, "My husband Carl died fifteen years ago. *Fifteen years.* How dare you come to me with these despicable hints and conjectures?"

"There'll be no conjecture at all when we exhume his body," Warrick said.

Eleanor glared at him, then at Catherine. "You can't do that," she said.

Catherine sighed. "We can, and we will," she said. "And you should know—if you don't already—that elevated traces of succinylcholine's chemical components remain in brain tissues indefinitely."

A moment passed. Another. Eleanor Samuels sat there looking at the CSIs, her features suddenly devoid of expression.

"I already asked what you wanted," she said. "Now tell me. Right out."

Catherine looked at her. "If we conclude Carl died of an undetected succinylcholine overdose, we'll have a trail that leads us straight from Layton to the deaths of Rose Demille and your first husband. I don't have any idea right now how much you knew or didn't know about Carl's death. But help us, and we'll inform the district attorney how valuable a witness you are to the case."

Eleanor sat very still.

And then, at last, sighed heavily.

"I'm not to blame for Carl . . . and what I know about his death, I only learned afterward," she said. "Leave me out of whatever you uncover, and I'll tell you everything I know."

It was almost half past midnight at headquarters. The place looked blue. Somehow, it always looked blue. Now and then, you might hear a couple of the uniforms whispering that it was probably because the CSIs had their fancy gizmos zapping ultraviolet radiation everywhere. But whatever the reason, when it got to be around midnight, it always seemed a deeper, bluer blue around HQ.

In the corridor outside the interrogation rooms, Catherine Willows, Warrick Brown, and Captain Jim Brass were waiting for showtime . . . which, more often than not, tended to start in the bluest of the blue hours around here. And though some occasionally muttered that Brass's frequent exposure to all this blueness was a contributing factor to his perpetually sunny (hardy-har-har) disposition, there was no real evidence supporting this claim.

There was, however, more than enough to form a solid basis for dragging Dr. Layton Samuels out of bed to question him about the murder of Nevada Rose Demille, something a couple of Brass's detectives had done on his orders a short while ago.

Glancing at his wristwatch, Brass figured they ought to be arriving with everyone's favorite plastic surgeon-cum-author-cum-daytime television fixture any minute now. In fact, he was wondering why the hell they hadn't already appeared. He turned to Catherine.

"What the hell do you think is going on?"

"Going on where?" she replied.

"Going on outside that's keeping those damned dragass *lunks* I sent to pick up Samuels from being here with him by now—"

The captain broke off as the vibrating cell phone in his pocket silenced him. He reached for it, flipped it open, and listened.

"Uh-huh," he said into the mouthpiece. "Give us five minutes, and don't be a second late."

Then he flipped the phone shut and looked at Catherine again. "They're here," he said. "Bringing Samuels out of the car."

She turned to Warrick. "Better get our other player ready for her cameo," she said. "Timing's everything."

He gave her a thumbs-up and hastened toward a waiting room a few feet down the corridor.

Exactly five minutes later, the pair of detectives dispatched to Samuels's residence came trotting around a bend in the corridor right beyond the waiting room. Sandwiched between them, bags under his eyes visible behind his glasses, the doctor looked none too pleased at having been hauled in by the police and bore little resemblance to the smiling, buoyant figure known to his loyal cult of TV viewers and book readers.

Watching him approach, Brass and Catherine traded glances.

Brass seemed on the precipice of annoyance. "Where's Warr—?"

He abruptly fell silent, yet another sentence aborted on his tongue as the about-to-be-mentioned Warrick Brown emerged from the waiting room with Eleanor Samuels, leading her directly across the path of her husband and the detectives.

Right on cue.

Seeing her there, Layton Samuels jerked up straight, halting as if his legs had turned to wooden posts. "Eleanor," he said, stunned. "Eleanor . . . what are *you* doing here?"

Warrick's hand on her arm, she stood a few feet in front of her husband, her face tight, meeting his astonished stare without response. Brass and the CSIs let the moment play out, wanting to give Samuels something to think about. Then Brass said, "Bring Mrs. Samuels to Interrogation Room A."

Warrick nodded, gently nudged Eleanor's arm. Her eyes lingered on her husband's for a moment before Warrick led her up the hall past Brass and Catherine.

After a silent three count, Brass turned toward the now very stunned and confused Samuels.

"Your lawyer's waiting for you in Interrogation Room B," he said, and nodded for the detectives to lead in the opposite direction from his wife.

A slim, attractive woman named Carole Eisling, Layton Samuels's pricey attorney, looked the diametric opposite of her client insofar as being ready for postmidnight dealings with law-enforcement personnel. Her sea-green eyes looked as sharp as an eagle's. Her hair and makeup were just so. Her thousand-dollar-plus Armani pantsuit was neat, crisp, and flatteringly tailored to her figure. Completing the image of prosperous efficiency, Eisling had put her beyond-expensive Salvatore Ferragamo briefcase on display on the interrogation-room table, positioning it smack dab between Samuels and herself on one side and Catherine and Brass on the other—presumably hoping it would impress the lowly LVPD peons into knowing their rightful places.

Brass wondered why it never occurred to these genius shysters out here in Vegas that all their showboat trappings only pissed cops off. Back in Jersey, someone like Eisling would have known better and gone for a more frumpish workaday look. But then again, this sure as shit wasn't Jersey. What else did you expect from a place symbolized by a sexy neon rodeo cowgirl?

"So, now that we're all gathered together,"

Eisling said, sounding appropriately chagrined, "how about somebody explaining why Doctor Samuels is here tonight, let alone at this absurd hour?"

When he considered what Samuels must be paying her, Brass was thinking she could have done a whole lot better than a clichéd opening question that didn't even merit a retort. He looked at Catherine, figuring she might as well take charge of things here.

With the obligatory Miranda rules cited and a video camera recording the interview, she did just that, explaining that Dr. Layton Samuels had been brought in for questioning about the death of Rose Demille and then proceeding to lay out the contradictions between his version of their supposedly passing acquaintance and certain information they'd come upon indicating he'd been less than candid.

Now came the familiar song and dance—a fusillade of obligatory objections from Eisling about the relevance of Samuels and Rose Demille's personal relationship, followed by Catherine's insistence that her client would benefit greatly if she stopped filibustering the interview and let the facts be aired.

Finally, if only perhaps temporarily, the spiffily clad attorney relented.

"Doctor Samuels," Catherine said at last, "why is it you never mentioned your separation from your wife when we spoke at your office?"

"It was a personal matter," he said. "I didn't see what it had to do with the reason you were there."

"Even though I'd asked about you having an affair with Rose Demille? And even though your wife has given a sworn statement that she filed for separation *because* of that affair?"

Samuels massaged the area above his nose with two fingers. "I told you," he said. "The separation was personal. And an embarrassment. I have a public reputation."

Brass looked across that table. His turn. "And you thought that reputation so important you'd lie to police conducting a murder investigation."

Eisling glowered, mouthed a few more objections, finally subsided, and whispered something in Samuels's ear.

"I wouldn't characterize it as a lie," the doctor said.

"Then how *would* you characterize it?"

"Protection of a brand name," Samuels replied. "My business has a clean image. I have a responsibility to my employees and corporate sponsors."

Silence. Brass passed the ball back to Catherine, who thought those words very reminiscent of Eleanor's defense of her happy-spouse charade. Two from the same mold.

"Just so we're clear," she said, "you're no longer denying your relationship with Rose Demille, is that correct?"

He looked at her. Rubbing the bridge of his nose now.

"Is something wrong, Dr. Samuels?"

He took a deep breath, exhaled, shook his head. "Nothing," he said. "Just a headache."

"I hope it isn't one of your migraines."

Samuels gave her a questioning look.

"Your wife told us you suffer from them," Catherine said. She pulled a transparent evidence bag out of her blazer pocket and set it on the table. Inside was the pill dispenser from Rose De-mille's dresser drawer. "We'd been wondering if this was something you might have misplaced."

Samuels looked down at the bag. Then back up Catherine. "Where did you get that?" he said.

"Rose's dresser. With some other odds and ends tucked away under some lingerie."

Samuels shook his head. "I don't recognize it," he said.

"You sure? Because Eleanor said she'd bought it for you a few months ago. Also, it contained traces of Verapamil and lithium . . . two of the medications you take when the headaches aren't too bad."

Samuels and Catherine commenced a staring contest.

"Did my wife tell you that as well?" he finally said.

"Well . . . Eleanor wasn't too happy when we informed her where we found the dispenser."

Not unexpectedly, that got Eisling practically

jumping out of her chair. "This is ridiculous!" she said heatedly. "You can buy pill dispensers like that anywhere . . . and if we started taking a count of everyone in Las Vegas who has chronic headaches—"

Catherine made a stop gesture and pulled the bag off the table. "I was just asking," she replied. Her eyes, however, remained on Samuels. "In case it jogged your memory about it being yours."

Samuels said nothing. Just sat there rubbing his brow.

"Would you like a glass of water?" Catherine said.

"No, thank you."

"You're sure? In case you need to take a pill for the headache," Catherine said. "Although I know you use third-line nasal medications—a DHE spray and intranasal cocaine drops—when the cycles become very severe. And that you sometimes have episodes so terrible you'll have a drink or two along with the medications."

"Eleanor again?" he said.

"Maybe she still worries about your health," said Catherine. "Mixing those drugs and alcohol is strongly contraindicated. It can have some very undesirable consequences. Intense emotional swings, loss of judgment, even sudden rages—"

"Okay, wait a minute, I'm really not liking where you're going with this!" Eisling said loudly.

Catherine glanced at Eisling, nodded, and

broke off, thinking she'd taken that tack far enough. "Doctor Samuels," she said, "I know you're very familiar with the anesthetic succinylcholine."

Samuels's eyes moved behind his lenses. A little upward flicker. If you were an expert on neurolinguistic eye movement, which Brass knew Catherine was, you knew you'd struck a nerve.

"Doctor Samuels . . ."

"I developed it. Pioneered its use. As I'm sure you also know . . . along with thousands of professionals in the surgical community."

Catherine looked at him steadily, watched him massage his temples with both hands now. Time to fire the heavy ammo.

"That's true, and I'm sure you're very proud of that accomplishment," she said. "But what all those doctors *don't* know—and might indicate something you wouldn't be too proud of—is that abnormally high levels of succinic acid and choline were found in Rose Demille's brain, a telltale sign of succinylcholine overdose—"

"Enough!" From Eisling.

"—and that our coroner discovered two pinpoint needle marks between Rose Demille's toes, where succinylcholine can be effectively administered—"

"I said *enough*—"

"And where only someone very experienced at using a syringe would leave them without having to poke around a few times."

"I'm telling you for the last time that I am objecting to these leading statements. And that we're going to call off this interview here and now if you continue—"

Now it was Brass who had enough. He shot Eisling a look. "Object all you want," he said. "But that won't change the fact that we've obtained an exhumation order for the body of Eleanor Samuels's first husband, Carl Melvoy. And that it's going to be tested for succinylcholine breakdown products that would still be highly detectable in his remains. And that we have a sworn statement from Mrs. Samuels that your client was having an affair with her while she was still married to Melvoy—and *finally*, that, while overmedicated for one of his migraines, he later admitted to her that he murdered Carl using an injection of succinylcholine—"

"That's it, we're done here!" Eisling started to reach for her fancy briefcase. "If I had any idea that we'd come here at this ungodly hour based on the vicious and baseless accusations of a spurned wife—"

"Dismiss those accusations if you want," Catherine said. "But they're part of a detailed account Eleanor gave me hours earlier at her apartment. And more important, they're part of the sworn statement she's giving a district attorney at this very moment."

Eisling pushed to her feet. "You've got some goddamned nerve not telling me about that in advance," she said, seething. She looked over at Samuels. "Layton, we're leaving."

He didn't budge. Just sat there with his head hanging between his hands, massaging his temples with the balls of his palms.

"We are terminating this interview right now, Layton," Eisling said, her tone frostily insistent. "If these people have the stones to apply for a formal arrest warrant based on circumstantial nonsense and hearsay, we can take it up again at some later juncture."

Samuels stayed put. Slowly lifted his head. Looked straight at Catherine. "Rose was my love," he said in a barely audible voice. "My obsession."

Eisling gave him a sharp glance. "Layton . . . as your attorney, I have to advise you that anything you say now can be—"

He waved her into silence. His eyes still on Catherine. A long moment passed that way. Eisling stood there, shook her head with resignation, and finally sat down as if the wind had gone out of her.

"If you loved Rose," Catherine said, "why did you kill her?"

Samuels kept looking at her, his eyes glistening now. "Our relationship was fine. *Perfect*, in fact." He paused. "The great ones, the innovative ones, those who allow themselves to think freely and without creative restraint . . . so many have had polyamorous relationships. Like Picasso, whose work you so admired. And Gauguin, my God, he had a virtual harem there in Tahiti." Another pause. "I shouldn't compare myself to those men. It sounds immodest. But what I've done for human bodies . . . how I've reshaped flesh and cartilage . . . it is a form of art, don't you think?"

Catherine said nothing for a minute, then, "You're saying it was okay with Rose if you saw other women?"

He expelled a long breath, rubbing his forehead. "I had no interest in anyone else. Rose was one of a kind. Nature had given her the physical attributes most women pay thousands, tens of thousands of dollars to replicate . . . that I can only aspire to achieve for them with my hands."

"So when you talk about being polyamorous . . ."

"I'm saying that I took pleasure from Rose having outside sexual relationships," Samuels said. "Knowing she slept with famous men . . . men who could have had any woman in the world but desired *her* . . . it's honestly difficult to explain the gratification it gave me. I suppose I'd have to equate it to the world of art again. To the great works I display on the video screens at my office. I can share the beauty of those masterpieces with others, but they know—and I know—that in the end, they belong to me."

"What changed things for you?" Catherine asked.

"Baker," Samuels said tightly.

"Mark Baker?"

He nodded. "Her affair with him was different. Everyone knew it had gotten serious. All you had to do was turn on the television to hear about it . . . to see them constantly out on the town together." He swallowed. "I knew I was losing her to that goddamned ballplayer. It was so obvious. And I just couldn't take it."

"So you plotted to kill Rose. And frame Baker for her murder in the process," Catherine said.

Samuels sat there in silence for several seconds, his eyes moist. "I'd *thought* about it," he said. "Call it a dark fantasy . . . we all have them, our poorer moments. But when she told me she was going to be with Baker for his birthday celebration . . . that she would have to see me afterward . . ."

"You felt like she'd become *his* work of art," Catherine said. "Like your places had changed and you were only the admirer."

More silence. Baker rubbing, rubbing, rubbing away at his forehead.

"It was the third-line medication," he said. "The night it happened . . . knowing I would have to wait until after they were together to see her . . . I'd taken too much of it, had a few drinks, and I made a terrible decision."

"To kill her while you were having sex," Catherine said. "Bring a succinylcholine injection to her house, tie her to the bed, pull out your needle to incapacitate her. And then use your own body weight to stop her from breathing."

Eisling looked at him. "Layton, please—"

"You thought of it just that night," Catherine persisted.

"Is what he's saying, yes," Eisling said. "This was not a premeditated act."

"Then what about the gym bag?"

This from Brass now. To break the rhythm of the interview, knock Eisling off stride before she could get too comfortable with whatever under-the-influence defense she was cooking up.

She did not look too pleased. "What are you talking about?" she said.

"Mark Baker's gym bag," Brass said. "Your client left it on the lawn to incriminate Baker. Make it seem like he'd dropped it running out to his car that night. But Baker told us he'd lost it weeks before. That he was sure he'd left it at Rose's place and looked for it there but couldn't find it."

"Because your client pilfered it from Rose's house," Catherine said, looking not at the lawyer but at Samuels to finish nipping her argument in the bud.

Samuels sat there staring back at her. Staring and massaging his head, rubbing so hard and constantly now Catherine could see the skin reddening under his hands. "'Still in my heart's a sorrow, I'd thought that time would fade, guess it's the kind of love you give, the kind of love we've made,'" he said.

Catherine tried not to look surprised.

"Nina Tyford," she said. "'Angel Heart' . . . I know the song."

Samuels looked at her for a long, long time with his moist, overbright eyes. Then, finally, he sighed.

"Most of us do," he said.

The break room. Half past two in the morning. Getting further and further from the witching hour and closer and closer to the hour of the wolf.

Walking over to the cafeteria-style table, Warrick Brown handed one cup of coffee to Catherine and set another down in front of Sara. Then he went back to the machine, filled his own cup, and lowered himself back into a chair at the table where the three had been comparing notes.

They all sipped quietly for a few moments.

"Nevada Rose," he said at last.

"The Nevada Rose," Sara said, nodding. "A once-in-a-lifetime scientific find and it looks like it'll be going to collateral heirs—some cousin or aunt living who knows where. And what happens to it is anybody's guess." She sighed. "Gloria Belcher was afraid that her sons would betray her . . ."

"And Layton Samuels that his *lover* would . . ." Warrick said.

"And meanwhile, those treacheries were only in the killers' minds," Catherine said. "Suspicion, jealousy, greed . . . the damn tragic thing is that it blinded *all* of them to loyalty . . ."

She let the rest of the sentence dangle in the air, seeing no need to go on.

When dealing with senseless murder, they could all very easily finish it for themselves.

About the Author

A native New Yorker, JEROME PREISLER has written more than twenty-five books of fiction and nonfiction, including all eight novels in the #1 *New York Times* bestselling *Tom Clancy's Power Plays* series.

Preisler is the co-author of *All Hands Down: The True Story of the Soviet Attack on the U.S.S. Scorpion*, a major work of narrative history recently published in hardcover by Simon & Schuster.

With his wife, Suzanne, he is the pseudonymous co-author of three comedic mysteries from Signet/Obsidian: *Scene of the Grime, Dirty Deeds,* and the forthcoming *Notoriously Neat.*

In 2005, Preisler began writing his column of baseball commentary, *Deep in the Red,* for the New York Yankees Sports and Entertainment Network's (YES) official website, YESNetwork.com.

He invites his readers to contact him at: www.JeromePreisler.com.

Play the Video Game
THE TRUTH IS YOURS TO DISCOVER

Featuring the voice and likenesses of the entire CSI cast

AVAILABLE NOW
at video game retailers everywhere.

www.csivideogames.com

CSIHE-4